Michael Blumlein

Twice nominated for the World Fantasy Award
Twice nominated for the Bram Stoker Award
ReaderCon Award for Best Collection
Shortlisted for the Tiptree Award

"Marvelous . . . important . . . a strong voice
and relentlessly truthful vision."
—*Fantasy and Science Fiction*

"A major talent on the horror scene."
—*Publishers Weekly*

"Blindingly brilliant . . . a genuinely great writer."
—Katherine Dunn, author of *Geek Love*

"Not for everyone. Only those who delight in splendid,
original thinking and rich, pyrotechnical language need apply."
—Harlan Ellison

"Michael Blumlein is a real original. . . . I don't think
anybody is going to be able to imitate him."
—Peter Straub

Thoreau's Microscope

plus

PM PRESS OUTSPOKEN AUTHORS SERIES

1. *The Left Left Behind*
   Terry Bisson

2. *The Lucky Strike*
   Kim Stanley Robinson

3. *The Underbelly*
   Gary Phillips

4. *Mammoths of the Great Plains*
   Eleanor Arnason

5. *Modem Times 2.0*
   Michael Moorcock

6. *The Wild Girls*
   Ursula K. Le Guin

7. *Surfing the Gnarl*
   Rudy Rucker

8. *The Great Big Beautiful Tomorrow*
   Cory Doctorow

9. *Report from Planet Midnight*
   Nalo Hopkinson

10. *The Human Front*
    Ken MacLeod

11. *New Taboos*
    John Shirley

12. *The Science of Herself*
    Karen Joy Fowler

PM PRESS OUTSPOKEN AUTHORS SERIES

13. *Raising Hell*
Norman Spinrad

14. *Patty Hearst & The Twinkie Murders: A Tale of Two Trials*
Paul Krassner

15. *My Life, My Body*
Marge Piercy

16. *Gypsy*
Carter Scholz

17. *Miracles Ain't What They Used to Be*
Joe R. Lansdale

18. *Fire.*
Elizabeth Hand

19. *Totalitopia*
John Crowley

20. *The Atheist in the Attic*
Samuel R. Delany

21. *Thoreau's Microscope*
Michael Blumlein

22. *The Beatrix Gates*
Rachel Pollack

THOREAU'S MICROSCOPE

plus

"Paul and Me"

and

"Fidelity"

and

"Know How, Can Do"

and more

Michael Blumlein

PM PRESS | 2018

"Paul and Me" first appeared in *Fantasy and Science Fiction*, October–November 1997

"Fidelity" first appeared in *Fantasy and Science Fiction*, September 2000, as "Fidelity: A Primer"

"Know How, Can Do" first appeared in *Fantasy and Science Fiction*, December 2001

"Y(ou)r Q(ua)ntifi(e)d S(el)f" first appeared (abridged) in *New Scientist*, December 20, 2014. A fuller version may be found in the collection *All I Ever Dreamed* from Valancourt Books, 2018.

"Thoreau's Microscope" with its preface is original to this volume. A slightly different version may be found in *Naming Mt. Thoreau* from Artemisia Press.

Thoreau's Microscope
Michael Blumlein © 2018
This edition © 2018 PM Press
Series editor: Terry Bisson

ISBN: 978-1-62963-516-3
Library of Congress Control Number: 2017964732

Cover design by John Yates/www.stealworks.com
Author photograph by Rudy Rucker
Insides by Jonathan Rowland

PM Press
P.O. Box 23912
Oakland, CA 94623
www.pmpress.org

10 9 8 7 6 5 4 3 2 1

Printed in the USA by the Employee Owners of Thomson-Shore in Dexter, Michigan • www.thomsonshore.com

CONTENTS

Paul and Me   1

Y(ou)^r Q(ua)^{n}tifi(e)^d S(el)^f 21

Thoreau's Microscope   29

Fidelity   49

Know How, Can Do   73

"A Babe in the Woods"   101
Michael Blumlein interviewed by Terry Bisson

Bibliography   113

Paul and Me
for Terry Parkinson

I FIRST MET PAUL in '71, the year I got out of college. I was bumming around the country, crashing in city parks and church basements, cadging food and companionship, avoiding the future. In keeping with the spirit of the times, I considered my carefree and unfettered existence both highly evolved and intrinsically righteous, when in truth I had no fucking idea. It didn't matter. My girlfriend was in New York City, living in a commune and doing guerilla theater. My ex-girlfriend was in Vancouver, BC, with her boyfriend, who'd fled the U.S. because of the draft. Those two women were ballast for me. In my imagination anyway, they were fixed points and gave me the security to do what I wanted in between.

I'd been in Bozeman a few days when I was busted for stealing a sandwich. After a night in jail, the judge threw me out of town. The first ride I got was headed to Seattle, but I wasn't ready for another city quite yet. I got out in Wenatchee, caught a ride to Carlton and two days later, a pack on my back and enough brown rice to last a week, was in the high country north of Lake Chelan.

There is nothing like the mountains to feel simultaneously large and small. Incomparably large, I should say, and insignificantly small. Distances are vast, yet life, because conditions are so exacting, is condensed. At the higher elevations the trees and wildflowers, the voles that skitter in and out of rocks, even the mosquitoes seem lilliputian. Which made Paul, at first glance, all the more striking.

He was kneeling by the edge of a stream, taking a drink of water. He had on those trademark jeans of his, the navy blue suspenders, the plaid shirt. From a distance he looked as big as a house, up close even bigger. Because of his size I expected him to be oafish, but he was nothing of the kind. He moved with remarkable grace, dipping his cupped hand delicately into the water then sipping from it with the poise of a lady sipping tea.

I was alone. It was July, and I had camped by a lake in a high meadow two valleys over. That morning I had gone exploring, following the drainage creek down as it fell through a boulder-strewn slope of fir and pine. An hour of walking brought me to the confluence of another, similar-sized creek, at which point the water picked up force. The trail leveled off for about a hundred yards, then dropped precipitously. This was the site of a magnificent waterfall, sixty, seventy feet high. Paul was at the far end of a deep pool carved by the water. His hair was dark and short, his beard trim, his lips as red as berries. Waves of reflected sunlight lit his face. He had the eyes of a dreamer.

The trail zigzagged down a granite cliff, coming out near the base of the waterfall. The noise of the falls was deafening and masked my approach. By the time he noticed me, I wasn't more than a stone's throw away. He stopped drinking, and a frown crossed his face. Quickly, this gave way to a stiff kind of courtesy, a seemliness and a handsome, though remote, civility. His public persona. I apologized for intruding and was about to continue on my way when he motioned me over.

Standing, he was thirty feet tall; kneeling, nearly half that height. His thighs when I first met him were as wide as tree trunks; his biceps, like mountains. As I drew near, he stood up and stretched, momentarily blotting out the sky. Then, as though conscious of having dwarfed me, he sought to put me at ease by sitting, or leaning rather, against a pine, which, though venerable, bent beneath him like rubber.

It was he who spoke first. His voice was deep and surprisingly gentle.

"Hello."

"Hello," I answered.

"Nice day."

"Incredible."

He looked at the sky, which was cloudless. Sunlight streamed down. "Doesn't get any better."

"Can't," I replied insipidly.

An awkward silence followed, then he asked if I came here often. I said it was my first time.

"You?" I asked.

"Every few months. It's a little hot for me this time of year. In the summer I tend to stay farther north."

I was wearing a T-shirt and shorts. He was in long pants and a flannel shirt with the sleeves partway rolled up. I suggested that he might be more comfortable in other clothes.

"I like to stay covered," he replied, which nowadays would mean he wanted to keep out of the sun but then was more ambiguous. I searched for something else to keep the conversation alive.

"So what made you come?" I asked. "South, I mean."

He shrugged. "I don't know. I had an urge."

I nodded. Urges I knew about. My whole last year of college had been one urge after another. Sex, drugs, sit-ins. As a life, it was dizzying. And now, having hiked into the high country with the lofty purpose of getting away from it all, of finding a little perspective, here I was talking to a man as tall as a tower. I felt as dizzy as ever, and I was humbled by the realization that the very impulsiveness I was running from was what had gotten me here to begin with. I also felt a little lightheaded, and thinking it might in part be a product of hunger, I took out a bag of peanuts. I offered him some, but he shook his head.

"I'm allergic to nuts. I blow up like a blimp."

This was news to me. Of everything I'd read or heard about him, nothing ever mentioned his being sick. I didn't know he could be.

"You don't want to be around," he said. "When you're used to pulling up trees like toothpicks and knocking off mountain tops like cream puffs, it's no fun being weak as a kitten. I'm a lousy invalid. Worse if I'm really sick. I had a fever once that started a fire and chills that fanned the flames so hot that half the camp burned down before the boys finally got it out. Then they had to truck in three days of snow to cool me off."

I could picture it. "One time I had a fever like that. It made me hallucinate. I was reading a book and the characters started appearing in my room. It was freaky."

"Mine was no hallucination," he said indignantly.

In those days, theories of the mind were undergoing a radical transformation. The word "psychotic" was being used in some circles interchangeably with the word "visionary," and people who hallucinated without drugs were held, at least theoretically, in high esteem. Obviously, Paul didn't see it that way, and I apologized if I'd offended him. At the same time it surprised me that he'd care.

"I have a reputation to uphold," he said.

It turned out he'd been getting bits and pieces of news from the lower forty-eight and knew, for example, about the Vietnam War, the protests, the race riots, women's liberation, and the like. Institutions were toppling everywhere. Traditions were in a state of upheaval. The whole thing had him worried, and I tried to reassure him.

"As far as I know, your reputation's intact."

"For now."

"Don't worry about it."

"No? How about what's happening to your President Nixon? He was loved once. Now look at him."

"Loved" seemed a strong word, and even then it was hard to believe Paul considered himself in the same category as a man on his ignominious way out of the White House.

"People are fickle," he said. "Times change, you don't, and what happens? All of a sudden you're a villain."

"Fame's a bitch," I said without much sympathy.

He gave me a look, and for an instant I thought I had gone too far. What did I know of impetuosity? He could squash me like an ant. But then he laughed, and the earth, god bless her, trembled too.

"I'm not famous, little man."

"Of course you are."

"I'm a legend."

"You're both."

He chuckled softly and shook his head, as though I were hopelessly naive.

We ended up spending a week together. He took me north to his logging camp, which lay in a valley between two wooded ridges. He kept Babe in a pen at the foot of the valley beside the river that drained it, and every afternoon for an hour or two the ox would dutifully lie on his side and dam up the churning water, creating a lake for the loggers' recreation. They bathed and fished, and the few who knew how swam. In winter, when the waters froze, they played hockey and curling.

Each morning we had hotcakes for breakfast. It was a ritual the men adored. Half a dozen of them would strap bacon fat to their feet and skate around the skillet, careful to avoid the batter, which was coming out of full-size concrete mixers with stainless steel flumes ten feet above their heads. I heard stories of skaters who'd fallen and been cooked up with the batter, dark-skinned men who'd been mistaken for raisins, light-skinned ones for blanched almonds. Nothing like that happened while I was there. Paul was sensitive to the reports of cannibalism and kept careful track of the skaters. If one fell, he'd quickly pluck him up, and if there'd been a skillet burn, he'd rub it with that same bacon fat they had on their feet. And that man would be offered the day off, though none of them ever took it for fear of being labeled a sissy.

After we had our fill of hotcakes, Babe would be led in and allowed to eat what was left. One morning I saw him sweep up ten stacks with a single swipe of his tongue, each stack the size of a silo. It took him less than a minute to stuff it all in his mouth, swallow it down, and bellow for more. It was a bone-shattering sound. When it came to hotcakes, the Babe was not to be denied.

"They'll be the death of him," said Paul. "But I don't have the heart to say no."

"I'm not sure he'd listen."

"He's quite reasonable about everything else. Works straight through from dawn to dusk. As many days as I ask. Never complains. Which makes it hard to deny him his one weakness. I feel caught. Too lenient if I let him eat, too strict if I don't."

"It's nice you care," I said. "But look. It's his choice. You're not responsible for what he does. Don't let him victimize you."

Paul looked at me as if I were daft, and maybe I was. On the other hand, maybe I was just ahead of my time.

Cupping his hand over his mouth, he leaned over and whispered in my ear, as though divulging a deep, dark secret. "He can't victimize anyone. How can he? He's an ox."

The men in the camp worked in shifts around the clock, but as a rule Paul didn't get started until after breakfast. But once he did, he was unstoppable. I saw him log the entire side of a mountain in a single morning, strip the trees, dress them, and have them staged to be hauled out by lunch. He carried a double-bladed ax that allowed him to chop two trees at once, and when he got going, he could fell a whole stand in the time it took for the first tree to hit the ground. He was a furious worker, with a wild spirit and a love for people. In response, people loved Paul, and they came from all over to work for him.

But he had a quiet side too, and a need for solitude. One evening the two of us took a walk over the ridge above camp and down into the next valley. The meadows were lush with lupine and Indian paintbrush. There was aspen and spruce and a lazy stream that flowed without a sound. We built a fire and gazed at the sky, which that far north dimmed but never completely darkened, so that only the brightest stars were visible. We shared our dreams. Being twenty-one, mine was to taste life. Paul's was more specific.

"I want to fall in love," he said.

I laughed, but he was serious. And wistful. And uncertain that he ever could.

To my mind he had already had. "You have a vision," I told him. "To tame nature, but with a spirit that refuses to be tamed. You do love. You love freedom. You love life."

"I want to love a man."

Timidly, his eyes sought mine. I could see how desperately his heart wanted to open. I was twenty-one and eager for experience. To put it another way, I was a rebel even against myself.

It was the first time I ever had sex with a man. Obviously, some things were beyond my capability. Afterwards, we joked about it. He called me "little tiger" and revealed how much he had always liked little people. His parents were small, as was his older sister. At first they thought Paul had a glandular condition and took him to prominent doctors and specialists who prescribed various nostrums, all to no

avail. They tried a Penobscot medicine man, who diagnosed posses-
sion by a powerful spirit and performed a daylong ceremony designed
either to rid or to honor this spirit, they were never quite sure which.
After that they gave up and just let the boy grow, which he did with
a vengeance. By six months he required a cradle the size of a ship; by
twelve he was plucking up full-grown trees and tossing them in the
air like matchsticks. His parents did their best to keep him out of
trouble, but he had a spirit that couldn't be harnessed. They had to
move frequently, and by the time Paul reached adolescence, they'd had
enough. Unwilling and unable to control him any longer, his parents
abandoned him in the forests of the Upper Peninsula, a deprivation to
which he attributed his craving to love and be loved. There were four
Great Lakes at that time. Paul's tears made the fifth.

Our meeting one another was one of those rare instances of two people's paths happening to cross at just the right time. We came together
with equal passion, equal need, and an equal degree of commitment. It
was intense, satisfying, and brief. Paul told me his deepest secrets and I
told him mine. Three days later we parted company, promising to see
each other again as soon as possible. Twenty years passed before we did.

Again it was summer. I had recently separated from my wife. This was
not my college sweetheart, the one who'd gone to New York to fight
the beast and topple the patriarchy, although we had been married
briefly. This was the woman I had met after law school. She was coming out of a bad relationship at the time, a crash-and-burn affair with
another woman, and was ready to try something new. I was new, and
we did famously for eight years, therapy for five, and now we were
trying separation. It was her idea, and I was having a lot of trouble
adjusting. A friend suggested I get away, and the first place I thought
of, or the first person, was Paul.

I took a plane to Wenatchee, picked up supplies and a car, then drove to Carlton. The town had grown. With the opening of the North Cascades Highway there were all sorts of new development. I saw no sign and heard no mention of Paul, and it crossed my mind that, despite his fondness for little people, this influx of commerce would not be to his liking. But I had a premonition that he'd be at that waterfall where we first met, a vague and vain idea that our lives were somehow running in parallel, that I would be on his mind as much as he was now on mine. It was a sixties kind of notion. Unfortunately, this was the nineties. He was not there, and he didn't come. I waited three days, then left.

I drove back to Wenatchee, turned in the car, and took a plane to Seattle. From there I headed north, on successively smaller planes, ultimately commandeering a four-seater Piper Cherokee that dropped me in Ross River, a few hundred miles south of the Arctic Circle in the Yukon. This was the vicinity of Paul's old camp, up in the Selwyn Range to the east, and here I heard mention of him, a whisper really, not much more. But a whisper was all I needed. The next day I was on my way.

It was August, and this was north. The days stretched on forever. I wandered in twilight, caught glimpses of moose and bear, fox on the run, geese in migration. I saw mountains decked in snow and a sky that shimmered with magnetism and light. But no Paul. His camp was empty and by the looks of it had been for years. The skillet that had cost old man Carnegie a year's output of steel was warped and covered with debris. The pen where Babe had slept was down, the field now overgrown with trees. I pitched my camp beside the creek he used to dam for the men, and cooked myself meals of desiccated sausage and freeze-dried eggs, all the while dreaming of hotcakes swimming in maple syrup. I took day hikes, resigning myself to the fact that this past, like my marriage, was over.

Then one day in a snowfield I saw footprints. Boot shaped, waist-deep, as long and wide as a wagon. That evening I found him.

He was sitting by a lake in a talus-sloped basin above tree line, absently tossing stones the size of tires into the water. The evening chill that had me in parka and mittens didn't seem to be affecting him. He was wearing what he always wore, though not in the way he always wore it. He was unkempt, his shirttails out, his boots untied. One of the legs of his pants was torn, and his beard, which I remembered as being neatly trimmed, was scraggly and matted.

The trail passed through scree, and the sound of shifting rock announced my arrival while I was still high above the lake. He looked up and frowned, as though unhappy at being disturbed. When he recognized who it was, the frown turned to a kind of puzzlement. He could have helped me down, but instead, he waited while I descended on my own.

It was a thrill to see him again. He said the same about me. But after the first flush of excitement our conversation lapsed. He seemed listless and preoccupied. I mentioned I'd been by the old camp.

"I saw you," he said.

"You saw me? When?"

"A couple of days ago."

My blood rose. "I've been looking for you nearly two weeks."

If this bothered him, he gave no indication of it. "I haven't been in the mood for people."

"What does that mean?"

"I'm depressed."

"You? C'mon. You're a mover. A shaker. You're a dreamer. You're the opposite of depressed."

"The world is leaving me. Everything I've ever loved is gone."

Gradually it came out. The logging industry had been in a prolonged slump. Demand for timber was a fraction of what it had been.

And most of the first-growth forests were gone, and the livable land cleared. Paul couldn't support a camp, and one by one the boys had left. Ole the Blacksmith, Slim Mullins, Blue-Nose Parker, Batiste Joe—all the old gang were gone. And then one day Babe had died. It was the hotcakes, just as Paul had always feared.

"He had an eating disorder. That's what the vet said. And I said, "All right, an eating disorder, so tell me what to do." But he didn't know, he'd never seen an ox like that.

"It got to be harder and harder to control him. The smell of me mixing the batter was enough to drive him crazy. One day he broke away and rushed the kitchen. The hotcakes were still in the oven, and he swallowed the whole thing at once, oven, burners, smokestack. Everything. Stupid ox. He burned to death, from the inside out."

"That's awful."

"Saddest day of my life," said Paul.

"When did this happen?"

"A year ago. Maybe two."

"Did you have someone to talk to? Someone to help you through?"

He looked at me with woe-begotten eyes. "Did. Then he died too."

Randy was his name. They were lovers, and Paul nursed him to his dying day. Buried him deep and built a mountain on top for a gravestone. It was less than a year since he'd passed away.

"Seems like yesterday," said Paul.

"I'm so sorry."

He sighed. "I keep wondering who's going to bury me."

"You planning on dying?"

"I dream of it sometimes. Is dreaming planning? You tell me."

A couple of years before, I'd had a bout of depression that responded nicely to a short course of Prozac. Fleetingly, I wondered how many truckloads of pills it would take to help Paul. I could hear the outcry from all those deprived by him of their precious drug, which made me weigh in my mind the good of the one against the good of the many, a quandary made all the more difficult by the one in this case having dedicated his whole life to the many. My brain was too weak to solve that riddle, and fortunately, Paul interrupted my attempt.

"I don't grow old the same as you," he said. "It may be a thousand years before I die. It may be never."

"Everyone dies."

"I'm as good as dead now. That's how I feel. The rivers are cut. The forests are logged. My friends are gone. Who needs me now?"

"I do," I said. "I need you."

He gave me a skeptical look. "You're being kind."

"I'm being honest. My wife left me. I know what it's like to feel unwanted and unloved."

Granted, my loss paled beside his own, but misery is misery and I needed to talk. It was all he could do to listen. His attention kept wandering, drawn inward by a self-absorption that, frankly, offended me. Talking to Paul was like talking to a pit, and finally I gave up.

The silence of the high country took over, normally a vast and soul-inspiring event. But neither of us was getting much inspiration. Paul was hopelessly withdrawn, and I felt angry at being cheated of my fair share of attention. I suggested, in lieu of conversation, a walk. Reluctantly, he agreed.

I had in mind a short stroll, something to stretch the legs and stir the blood, a constitutional. We ended up on a three-day trek to the Arctic Circle and back. Most of the time I rode on his shoulders, which he said made him feel useful. The scenery was magnificent, the land uninhabited by man. We had snow and wind and skies the color of gemstones. I thought frequently of my wife and the early years of our relationship. I missed her. The vast and untrammeled beauty in that deserted land made my heart ache to have her back.

Paul seemed happy enough to be on the move, but when we returned, his spirits again plummeted. I stayed with him a day or two more, listening to his troubles, suppressing my own, growing impatient and even resentful while trying to appear otherwise. Eventually, I couldn't stand it anymore.

"I have to get back," I told him.

He nodded morosely, then gave me a penetrating look. "Why did you come?"

It was the first genuine interest he had shown in me since I arrived.

"To see you," I answered.

"Why?"

I thought about it. "I had an urge," I said at length, flashing a smile. "Remember urges?"

"I do. Yes. Vividly."

He gave me a look, beseeching I thought, as if he wanted something, then fell silent. As the silence grew, I began to feel defensive.

"I didn't come to replay the past, if that's what you're asking." I drew a breath. "I'm not gay, Paul."

"Is that why you came? To tell me that?"

This irritated me. "I came because I needed a friend."

He seemed to find this amusing. "And have I been?"

"It's been a rough time for you. I understand. Yes. Of course you've been a friend."

"Of course." He made a parody of the words. "Just so you know, you haven't. Not at all. You're patronizing and self-serving. You breeze in at your whim, you breeze out. You don't care." He made a motion with his hand of sweeping me away. "Go away, little man. Enjoy your little life and your little troubles. Your little country. Go away and do me the pleasure of not coming back."

***

That was '91. It was the culmination of a bad stretch of time. Two years before, I had turned forty and Sheila, my wife, forty-one. We had put off having a family because that's what our generation did, put off certain commitments in order to indulge others. We traveled. We became enlightened. We fought injustice. We didn't have children because we were children, children of the new age. And then when we were ready, we couldn't. The equipment just wasn't up to snuff. Sperm without heads, ovaries without eggs. It was pathetic. We'd grown old before we'd even grown up.

We went to doctors. Took tests, hormones, injections. Tried the turkey baster, the baking soda douche, the upside-down post-coital maneuver. We charted temperature and checked mucous, fucked on schedule and the rest of the time not at all. Were we having fun? Sure we were. And just to emphasize the point, we upped our therapy to three times a week.

And those, believe it or not, were the good times. The bad started after we visited the baby broker. Met her in an unfurnished tract home on an empty street in a white-bread suburb of Sacramento. Our hopes were high, but one look at her told us it was all wrong. She was a right-to-lifer, smug and self-possessed. She marched outside abortion clinics and hurled insults while on the side she gave Christian guidance to unwed mothers. She had a photo album of all the children she had placed and showed it to us like a lady selling Tupperware. Beautiful babies with angelic faces, flawless parents with milky complexions and award-winning smiles. She advised us to print up a thousand leaflets and pass them out in parking lots. Stand on street corners with placards announcing our need. Beg for babies.

She told us, in essence, that we were to blame for our childlessness and if the Lord willed us to be parents, then and only then would we be.

It just wasn't our thing.

We paid her her two hundred dollars, then went home and puked. Two months later, Sheila moved out.

The shock of it sent me reeling, as though gravity had suddenly ceased. I cried on and off for weeks, couldn't get a purchase on things, felt disoriented and racked by a sense of guilt, failure, and self-doubt. In retrospect, that had been my purpose in visiting Paul, to restore some degree of proportion and balance to my life. He was, if nothing else, a man with his head on his shoulders and his feet on the ground. Mr. Dependable. Or so I thought. When he turned out to be such a downer, when he gave me nothing, when in the end he accused me of being a fraud, I felt betrayed.

On my return from that ill-conceived trip, I threw myself into work, which at the time was malpractice litigation. Perhaps in reaction to being hurt myself, first by Sheila, then Paul, I went after those hospitals and doctors who had hurt others. That most of these injuries were unintentional was beside the point. Errors are errors, and in matters of law it makes no difference that all of us are guilty. I sued on behalf of a woman who'd lost her baby at birth, a man who'd lost an eye, a teenager with brain damage after being struck in the head by the plaintiff, his father. We got a huge settlement for that one, and a few months later we got a fat check in a sexual impropriety verdict against a surgeon who'd been fondling his anesthetized patients. That case made the newspapers, and my wife, who at the time was teaching a course on sexual harassment at the local community college, called to offer her congratulations. It was a little more than a year since we had separated, an anniversary that we had carefully failed to observe. The date now safely past, we felt capable of meeting for dinner. Sheila, I have to say, was ravishing. Evidently, she felt the same about me. We couldn't keep our hands to ourselves, nor our laughter, nor delight. One thing led to another, and we ended up spending the night together. Three weeks later she called to say she was pregnant.

Now we have a two-year-old son. He's got the build of an ox and the temperament, alternately, of a rabbit and a mule. Lately, he's been constructing tall and elaborate towers of blocks that he subsequently reduces to rubble with a kick. In other games he is equally omnipotent, digging a hole in the sandbox, for example, which he then fills with water and proclaims an ocean, before draining it completely a minute later and naming it, triumphantly, a desert.

Paul was once like that, making lakes with his footsteps, straightening rivers with a tug of his massive arms, causing tidal waves when he sneezed. A creator and a destroyer. I've been thinking of him a lot lately.

The anger and hurt I felt after that last visit lessened with time, and as sometimes happens, my feelings actually reversed themselves, so that I started to blame myself and not him for being insensitive and unsympathetic. Now, with a good marriage, a happy child, a successful job—in short, with everything going my way, I felt up to the task of braving whatever resentment he might still harbor toward me. I wanted to make peace.

This time I called first. Got the phone number of the Ross River post office and asked the postmaster, who'd lived there his whole life, if he'd had wind of Paul. He hadn't, not in a year or two. He told me to try farther north, up around Mayo, but instead I called Carlton, where, after getting nowhere with one lackey after another, I ended up talking to the head of the Chamber of Commerce. He knew nothing of Paul, although he had heard reports, strictly off the record, of some sort of creature on the loose. A Bigfoot, the locals were saying, which he discounted as a hopelessly crass ploy by the environmentalist cabal to keep the latest ski resort from being built. Bigfoot, he explained, had been listed by some joker in the state senate as an endangered species. It was a pretext to stymie development. What had happened could have been the result of almost anything.

I asked what he was talking about.

"Oh," he said offhandedly. "A thirty-foot anchoring tower disappeared from the top of one of our mountains the other day. Reappeared the next day in the same spot, but upside down."

That sounded promising. I asked if he had any theories.

"It's been a heavy winter." There was a pause on the line. "You one of those ecology nuts?"

I assured him I was not. "I'm looking for my friend. It's strictly personal."

There was another pause, as if he were calculating whether my actually finding this person would be to the Chamber's benefit or not. Apparently, he decided it would be, because he told me by all means to come up and have a look.

That was in May. In July I took a week off work, promising Sheila to be careful and my son Jonah to bring back a present, and headed to the mountains west of Carlton and north of Lake Chelan.

It had, indeed, been a heavy winter. There was still snow across many of the trails, and the streams and rivers were running full. Penstemon and buttercup bloomed in the meadows, and the young trees looked plump and green. I made camp the first night near the base of a burned-out pine and the next day hiked to the waterfall. There was a level spot about fifty feet from the water's edge where I pitched my tent, laid out my bedroll, and promptly fell asleep.

When I woke, Paul was standing in the pool. He was facing upstream, so that I saw him in profile. It was truly a shock.

His arms, once so massive, were the size of twigs; his legs, barely as big as saplings. His beard was moth-eaten, his skin blotchy and pale. He splashed some water on his naked chest and neck, then cupped his hands to get a drink from the waterfall itself. But he lacked the strength, so that the force of the water kept pushing his arms away. He tried again and again, and then for a minute he seemed to forget what he was doing. When he remembered, he sank to his knees and drank directly from the pool. Then he crawled onto the shore, at which point he caught sight of me.

His eyes narrowed, then he quickly tried to cover his naked body with his hands. Just as quickly, I turned away to give him his privacy.

When he had dressed, he told me I could turn around. I apologized for taking him by surprise.

He gave a little shrug. "It's all right. I expect I'm quite a sight."

I found myself nodding. "What's happened to you?"

"Clothes don't fit too well, do they?" Grinning, he hitched up his suspenders. "Good thing I don't wear a belt. My pants would be down by my ankles. Then where would I be?"

It was a feeble attempt at humor and took more breath than he had. Several seconds passed before he got it back.

"What was I saying?"

"Your pants . . ."

He glanced at them and brushed away some dirt. Then he looked at me. "I'm dying."

"That's ridiculous. You can't die."

He pointed to a purple lump on his arm as big as a grapefruit. And another under his beard. "They're all over. It's how my lover died. Now I will too."

This was unacceptable to me. "Have you been to doctors? Have you seen anyone for this?"

"What would they do? Give me medicine? I know about that. It's in short supply as it is. And besides, I don't mind dying. I've been alive long enough. Longer than I care to be."

"Legends don't die," I stammered.

He smiled, a look less of the sun as it used to be and more now of the moon. A reflective smile. A sad, sweet one.

"It's too cold for me up north. That's why I'm here. Stay with me. Will you?"

I couldn't refuse. And am forever glad that I didn't. I stayed with him more than a week, almost two, sending word to Sheila through a passing hiker that I'd be delayed. After a few days, we moved to the high country, which was deserted. Paul was forgetful but otherwise remarkably sunny, an effect, I suppose, of the illness, although I couldn't ignore the other truth, which was that he had lived his life and now was ready, even eager, to die. He was also weak as a kitten, and one morning he fell while we were traversing a snow field and ended up sliding down the icy slope into a glacial lake at the bottom. He laughed at his ineptitude, but the next day he developed a cough. The following morning it was worse, and by that evening he could barely breathe.

We were in the drainage of a semicircle of tall peaks, at the foot of which was a meadow fed by snowmelt. He dragged himself there, then collapsed, face up, eyes closed. Between labored breaths, he asked to be cremated, his ashes scattered. He whispered something else I didn't hear, then fell silent.

I made a pallet by his head and to pass the time told him stories, tales of Paul Bunyan and Babe, the Blue Ox, how they plowed the land into valleys and rivers, moved the mountains and logged the forests. I told him the story of the Blue Winter, and the popcorn blizzard that froze the cattle. And the one about the killer bees, and the carving of Puget Sound. Some time later he opened his eyes.

"I have loved," he said, with emphasis on the have, as though he were debating some point, or answering a question. And then he died.

It took me two days to gather enough wood for the pyre. The blaze lit the sky. And his ashes, when they cooled, made such a pile that to scatter them took three days and a wind out of Heaven, and as far away as Spokane the sky turned dark and people spoke of a new volcano, though no one ever found a trace.

Y(ou)^r Q(ua)^{n}tifi(e)^d S(el)^f

YOU WANT TO BE healthy. You want to know about yourself. You want to be happy. You need to know about yourself. You want to live a long, productive life. It starts and ends with yourself.

How long does it take to get going on an average day? What's your boot-up time? The norm is a bell-shaped curve, much broader than you, personally, would like to see. You'll want to narrow your own curve down. You'll observe what effect this has, right on down the line. Take your heart, for example. How many times does it beat in a day? Depends on the day. Depends on the heart. But on average 86,400. That's 8.6×10^4. For each chamber of your heart (4 in all), it's the same number. But for all 4 chambers combined it's 4 times as many beats a day. That's 34.4×10^4 (or 3.4×10^5), a substantially higher number. You narrow your curve, that number might climb as high as 4.2×10^5. That's a lot of beats. Not too many, mind you. Your heart is built to beat. You'll race out the door. Good job!

Your body is a temple. You have a duty to know how it stands. Your friends who visit the temple, who hang around on the steps, and the lucky ones invited inside, have a right to know the roof won't collapse and the walls won't crumble, they have a vested interest in knowing the building is sound.

How much have you eaten today? How many calories? How many servings? When you stood on the scale this morning, what did it say? Tip of the week: avoid the metric system. Use pounds instead. They melt away so much faster than kilograms. How much faster? More than twice as fast (2.2, to be precise). You'll have already knocked off a full pound before you've shed even half a kilo.

Not trying to lose? Trying to bulk up instead? Same deal. Quicker results with pounds. Even quicker (by a factor of 2^4) if in place of lbs., you use ounces. Good for the forces of change. Good for your head.

How many steps, on average, do you take per day? You know the length of your stride. You know the number of strides between bedroom and kitchen, kitchen and bathroom, bathroom and bed. You know the number of stairs you go up and down each day. You know how many times you shift on your feet while standing at work. How many times you walk down the hall. Your wristband monitors the distance you travel. It measures how many calories you burn. It counts the steps between here and there.

36% of you are stepping right now. 2 out of 3 will be reading this as you do: reading while exercising is a time-honored way to maximize your daily throughput score. 68% of you readers will be riveted by the material. 18% will be nodding off. Be sure to keep your monitor on when your eyes drift closed, whether you're at the desk, on the bus, on the couch, or in bed. You'll want to keep track of the distance you log during sleep: in visits to the kitchen, for example, the bathroom, or to check the front door. If you're a sleepwalker—and a lucky 13% of you are—you'll want to know the duration of your travels, and the average length of your stride. A shuffling walk, you'll note, burns fewer calories than a steady march; a steady march, less than a taut, suspenseful pacing. But all add to the daily count, and when you wake and see what you've unknowingly accomplished, you'll feel as if it's Christmas day.

No need to dwell on this. You're already counting your steps. You're keeping track of everything you put into your body. You're watching your weight like a hawk. But are you also watching your height?

What shoes are you wearing? Are you tracking their effect on your heart rate, your blood pressure, your mood? How do flats compare to pumps? Shit-kickers to stilettos? Sandals to sneakers?

71% of you raise your height with footwear between 2.6 and 4.7 cm 76% of days. (Female to male discordance is less than you might think.) Of these, 62% will volunteer an opinion or otherwise assert yourself without being prompted. Below 1 cm and above 7 cm of additional height (or *lift*), meekness and faux-meekness predominate by a 2-to-1 margin.

Height affects your mood, and it affects your worldview. You know this. 82% of you average lifters have experienced a more positive outlook, as measured by a shift in the power axis of the Myers-Briggs. 68% have noted an increase in appetite. 77% of you have craved to do something you've never done before.

Your altimeter will take care of the numbers; all you have to do is jot down your mood. Once or twice every hour, which you're doing anyway. You're keeping track of how you feel (what some people call, ambiguously, your "emotional state"). The purpose, of course, is to increase your level of happiness.

Take your bowel movements, for example. You won't simply be monitoring the number you have in a day. Or a week. You won't merely be measuring their weight, circumference and length. You'll already know to the minute how long you sit on the toilet (if you're a sitter), but what you'll want to know—what you'll be asking yourself, and documenting—is how do you feel? Should you be stretching the time out? Limiting it? Are you straining? What does your manometer say? How much TP do you use? How many sheets per wipe? Per sitting?

And what effect, if any, does this have on your so-called emotional state?

And afterwards, when you're cleaning up, do you glance in the mirror? Do you like what you see? 27% do; 43% don't. 53% will steal another look—in the same mirror, or a different one later. Of these, half will experience a flutter in their chest. Flutterers live, on average, 168 days longer than non-flutterers. Which are you?

It's your business to be aware, and awareness starts with yourself. Are you breathing? Well of course you're breathing, but are you breathing appropriately for the situation? Are you breathing optimally? During sleep do you slow to a felicitous 3 breaths per minute? During sex what's your maximum upgrade? Do you gasp? Is the gasp authentic (A) or manufactured (M)? Females have a high ratio of (M) gasps: nearly 3 to 1, when compared to (A) ones. Males are the reverse, but curiously, the ratio is changing. There's value, it appears, in a simulated, fraudulent gasp: 22% of males attest to this, as compared to a mere 8% a decade ago.

(A) gasps and (M) gasps have varying effects on health, but all gasps are salutary. (Survival benefit is clear on the Kaplan-Meier grid.) They may leave you starved for air, but no worries. You'll get your breath back soon. Don't forget to note exactly how soon. If you're still wearing your wrist monitor, this will be measured automatically. If you haven't lied about your weight, you'll know how many calories you've consumed. You'll be able to compare this number with the calories used by your friends and acquaintances. You'll know exactly where you stand.

If you're a guy, you'll want to know the volume of your wad. You might be interested to learn you're tossing out, on average, 60 million sperm per milliliter (that's 300 million per teaspoon, or 230 billion per gallon), each time you let fly. If you're an average man, with a 3.5 ml package, that's 210 million of the little guys. You might find this wasteful. Alternatively, you might be pleasantly surprised.

If you're a gal, you'll be monitoring your vaginal blood flow, elasticity and humidity. You'll note how little these correlate with other signifiers of the ideal mate you carry in your head. Experience has taught you that heat in the basement does not automatically translate into heat in the penthouse. Thought is the proverbial wild card, unlike in the male of the species, where the combination of penile vasocongestion and stiffness are 91% effective in rendering thought a lost cause.

There's a riddle here (beyond the riddle of the sexes), a little mathematical brainteaser. Do you see it? Yes. The integral of vaginal blood flow times elasticity divided by gasps per minute defines a Fibonacci sequence. Surprised? Don't be. Is a nautilus surprised by its spirals? A daisy by its petals? A starfish by its arms? You're a creature of our one, beautifully syncopated, beautifully mathematical universe. All living things conform to the same essential living processes. All things, living or not, obey the fundamental principles of existence.

If you exist—whether or not your existence is noticed (61% of the time it is), whether you yourself detect it or not—you are exquisite. At any given time, a sobering 77% of you will not share this experience. On a scale of 1 to 10, where 10 is absolute, self-conscious, self-absorbed bliss and 1 is self-loathing, self-repulsion, and infinite despair, the mean score is 5.3. Some of you will be aghast at this, but most will be cheered, as you recognize, (1), your score is substantially higher; and (2), there's ample room for self-improvement.

You will, of course, be wearing oxygen sensors. This goes without saying. The sensors allow you to move—in real-time—from poorly oxygenated areas, such as dance clubs and coal mines, to well-oxygenated ones, such as rainforests and augmented O_2 infusion cubicles, or the reverse, if you choose. Carbon dioxide sensors are also recommended: CO_2 can reach near-toxic levels in mere conversation, as other people, your friends or co-workers, for example, surround you and have the audacity to exhale.

Take-home message: you're not alone in the world. Duh. You're a Boolean entity, every day more Boolean than the day before. Worldwide, the interactive overlap is accelerating at the rate of 5.4%. 3 out of 4 people know more about 2 out of 3 people than they did 4.2 days ago. 5 out of 9 know more, but less than they should. 6 out of 7 are happy on 1 out of 2 occasions. 4 out of 5 on 1 out of 3. 9 out of 10 wish things were better. 3 out of 8 try to make them better. 2 out of 9 have no idea what's going on.

You'll recognize this latter group. They'll be looking dazed and overcooked. If you have a humane bone in your body (and where else would it be), now is the time to use it. You have no obligation to help, but you'll want to. The fold of helpers is growing. 8.4×10^6 at last count. There's a movement afoot. No fee to join. Nothing to sign. No leaders. You'll want to be a part, you'll say.

Here you'll pause. In 3–4 seconds (average 3.3) you'll give the secret sign. Then the secret handshake. You'll want to be careful. You know what can come of extending yourself. You understand the risks of contact of any sort.

You may decide to hold off on the handshake. You may choose to smile instead. Not a full-blown, 43-muscle smile but not an excessively stingy one either. A 35–40%, invitational smile. Consuming a nothing-to-sneeze-at 2.9 joules of energy, and spreading a proportionate amount of caloric encouragement. You'll observe what effect this has, and from here decide what to do next. The odds are 9 to 5 you'll make the right choice.

You can improve the odds by waiting another 4 minutes before proceeding. This may seem strange to the other party, your standing there without saying or doing anything. Your smile will probably have faded. Your eyes may have taken on a glaze. You may appear distracted or uninterested.

Nothing could be further from the truth.

You're running a risk-benefit analysis.
You're monitoring your 33 most vital signs.
Uninterested? Hardly.
Distracted? Please.
You're immersed.

Thoreau's Microscope

A Preface

About two years ago a small group of us—writers and artists primarily, including the poet Gary Snyder, and the novelist Kim Stanley Robinson—went on an expedition to the California High Sierras. We had two things in common: our love of the mountains, the Sierras in particular, and a feeling that something was missing from them.

In the Sierras every mountain is named after someone, a famous explorer, or scientist, or naturalist, but none is named after, arguably, the greatest American naturalist of all, Henry David Thoreau.

The purpose of our expedition was to rectify this. We hiked for two days, camped overnight at a high alpine lake, and the following morning scaled the previously unnamed Peak 12,691 and christened it Mount Thoreau. Then we came down and partied.

At the celebration the poets among us read their poetry; the prose writers, their prose; the artists and photographers showed their art. I spoke about Thoreau's exuberance, his rebelliousness, his privilege, and his incredible powers of observation. I quoted from his wonderful description of warring armies of ants in Walden, then read a few lines about a less martial ant encounter from one of my own stories.

The celebration ended, and we all went home, but I wasn't done. I wrote a second essay, drawing on both personal history and a lifetime as a scientist. I call it

Thoreau's Microscope

-1-

It was not Thoreau who got me to the mountain. I knew of him of course, and was soon to learn much more, but at the time knew little directly of the man and his writings. What I knew was by reputation and mostly secondhand, from the writings and admiration of others, much as I knew Darwin, who already had a fine mountain named after him, and whose *On the Origin of Species* Thoreau read and studied avidly. Or as I knew Louis Agassiz, the great Swiss glaciologist, ichthyologist, and founder of the Harvard Museum of Comparative Zoology, who befriended Thoreau and to whom Thoreau sent specimens from the ponds and streams of Concord in order to supplement his meager income; Agassiz also has a fine mountain named for him, a bit south of the one we were after. As does Emerson, a hop, skip, and jump north, spitting distance in Sierra terms, though the spit would have to cross a deep canyon. The unnamed peak that was our target, Peak 12,691 according to the USGS, was a smidge shorter than Mt. Emerson (as Thoreau himself was than his friend and mentor), but also a smidge more colorful. Its rock is layered into dark and light bands, and at certain times of day, dawn for example, when the air turns buttery and thick, the contrast is striking.

I've been coming to these mountains, the Sierra Nevada, for more than fifty years. I'm drawn to them by what draws most of the mountain climbers I know: the hugeness, the grandeur, the feelings of austerity and fullness they evoke, of being stripped of nonessentials, of freshness and first things. We're drawn by the *rock,* which is rough, smooth, abrasive, jagged, glinty, mineral-rich, multi-colored, and multi-sized—boulders tossed around like knuckle bones; buttresses and slabs thrust upward like titanic fists. Fractured and occasionally crumbly; mostly monolithic and unmovable, yet always on the move. Being in the mountains is being in the presence of an elemental force, where everything—especially everything above tree line—is reduced to fundamental principles, where complexity becomes simple, even transparent, and the spirit soars.

Thoreau deserved a mountain named for him; no one in our party disagreed. Ironically, though, he wasn't what we'd think of as a man of the mountains. There *are* no mountains east of the Mississippi like those to the west. He visited the White Mountains, but save for these trips, and his one ascent—and astonishing account of this ascent—of Mt. Ktaadn, he was a man of rolling hills, meadows, and forests. The bedrock where he lived is far older than the rock of the Sierras and, with few exceptions, more deeply hidden and harder to see. He made close observations of water, of course, and snow, and rain, but for the most part his eye was on the organic world of living things.

He had the obsessive mind and habits of a scientist. He was detailed in his observations and punctilious in writing them down. He carried a pencil and diary on his daily walks, a spyglass for looking at birds, a sturdy book to press plants, a jackknife, some twine, and a microscope.

Linnaeus, the father of modern taxonomy, who described and classified well in excess of 10,000 animals and plants, carried sheets of paper to press plants on his many expeditions. John James Audubon, hunter, naturalist, artist, and general lover of life, who witnessed firsthand the wanton destruction of hundreds of thousands of seabird eggs by eggers off the Labrador coast, prompting him to consider in horror the unthinkable at the time—that nature could be and would be exhausted if such behavior persisted—was never without a spyglass. Thoreau, along with his friend Agassiz and a growing number of geologists, botanists, biologists, and seaside hobbyists, carried a microscope.

The best microscopes of the time were made in Germany, although Spencer in Upstate New York, whose first catalogue appeared in 1840, was rapidly closing the gap. A hundred and fifty years earlier, before scientists and enthusiasts were training their scopes on the invisible world, before Thoreau was looking at tree rings, pond scum, mushroom caps, and the shiny, chitinous armor of red and black ants, Antonie Van Leeuwenhoek was looking through his homemade, single-lensed, one-by-two-inch, flattened brass microscope and seeing a little swimming thing he called an "animalcule." It was the first recorded glimpse of microscopic animal life.

Leeuwenhoek's microscope was a revolution in the age-old art and science of optics and microscopy. It was able to magnify objects an astounding 300 times, and people all over Europe, including Leibniz and Peter the Great, beat a path to his door in the hopes of going home with one. He was visited repeatedly by members of the Royal Society in London, who wanted to learn the secret of this radical new instrument, which rested in how he made the tiny lens, and which Leeuwenhoek steadfastly refused to reveal.

As an adolescent, Leeuwenhoek apprenticed in a linen-draper's shop, and in manhood opened a shop of his own. He also worked as a land surveyor and a wine assayer. Over the course of his long career he held several key (and remunerative) municipal posts in his native Delft. He knew Johannes Vermeer, a fellow Delftian, whose will he executed, and hobnobbed with important civic leaders. He came to science somewhat late in life, which perhaps explains why he still possessed, in addition to the requisite inquisitiveness, the three signature virtues of a scientist: he was humble, he was honest, he was generous. He wrote upward of 500 letters to the Royal Society during his lifetime, freely sharing all he had learned of fleas, aphids, spermatozoa, red corpuscles, capillaries, plant and muscle fibers, bacteria, and more. But, despite repeated pleas, he never divulged the secret of his superior lens-making ability (a lens barely bigger than the head of a pin), for before he was ever a scientist, and a darling of the scientific community, he was a successful merchant and businessman, with a businessman's understanding of supply and demand, and the particular power of proprietary information.

Thoreau, I suspect, had he lived 150 years earlier, would have had problems with this. Had he lived in Holland, which is not much larger than the state of Massachusetts, he probably would have known Leeuwenhoek. Their paths might have crossed in Delft, which was a bustling metropolis of art and commerce, and which Thoreau would have visited, though never for long—the noise and bustle would have driven him back to the woods. Leeuwenhoek, who was like Agassiz in being a public figure, with an outgoing, public personality, might have made him long for a simpler and quieter life, though chances are Thoreau would have liked the man. Certainly he would have had great respect for Leeuwenhoek's industry and inventiveness. He would have loved seeing his workshop, where science and nature collided, and nature was not unduly harmed, but revealed. He would have marveled at Leeuwenhoek's animalcules and the device that made them visible, that made the invisible world suddenly and miraculously spring to life. Like everyone else in Europe he would have wanted this device.

Despite his noble insistence on simplicity and self-reliance, Thoreau owned things he could not possibly have made himself. A compass, for one. (He used it for surveying.) His spyglass, with its finely ground lenses and sturdy manufactured metal cylinder. His microscope. Surely he understood that progress did not come without a price tag.

But he would have hated the secrecy. Science and its practitioners had a higher purpose than profit. Innovation required perspiration, sure, but inspiration too, and how could you put a number to something that was born of, and owed its value to, the human spirit? You couldn't, and it was wrong to try. Freedom of thought carried a responsibility, a social responsibility, especially when that thought led to something of value. You've discovered a new way to see? A way that not only magnifies, not only deepens, but *revolutionizes* what we know of life? Uncool to keep it to yourself. Why be stingy when nature is not? An economic saboteur, that was Thoreau, one in a long tradition of saboteurs, utopians, and anarchists who believed in open source.

Thoreau is the classic case of the poet-scientist, the ardent, emotive, woolgathering, metaphor-loving, silver-tongued, freewheeling and opinionated artist trapped in the body of a sober, rational, level-headed and dispassionate materialist. And vice versa. I say trapped, but it's more a cohabitation, each "half" or "side" infiltrating, illuminating, at times confusing, and regularly delighting the other. Harmony, synergy, conflict, mutual enlargement: this is the result of such a mind, an ecology of the highest plane. When he's not poor beyond words, down in the dumps, and utterly without confidence, the poet-scientist is happy as a clam, because he knows he sees things as they truly are, as much as humanly possible. Sight, true sight, brings a kind of ecstasy. The poet-scientist is that lucky man or woman who gets to experience the ecstasy of science, which is the ecstasy of order, everything-in-its-place, logic, reason and reproducibility, as well as the ecstasy of poetry, of art, which is the ecstasy of plunging into the unknown, of being swept away, the ecstasy of surrender. The poet-scientist is attuned to mysteries, which he seeks to unravel, not forgetting there's a time for thought and a time to turn off thought, a time to open the senses and revel in mystery and the divine. When he steps out the door, whatever the weather, whatever the season, life is a miracle to him. No one has it better than the poet-scientist.

Late in his life, Thoreau had this to say about microscopes: "Science is inhuman. Things seen with a microscope begin to be insignificant. So described, they are as monstrous as if they should be magnified a thousand diameters. Suppose I should see and describe men and houses and trees and birds as if they were a thousand times larger than they are! With our prying instruments we disturb the balance and harmony of nature."

Fair enough. Science *is* inhuman, perfect science that is, if there is such a thing. Inhuman in the sense of unfeeling, impersonal, unprejudiced and amoral. With our instruments we *do* pry. With or without instruments we humans are disturbers par excellence.

Yet here we are. And there Thoreau was, after a lifetime of looking, and looking closer, saying it was time to stop. He died three years later, almost to the day, of tuberculosis, which he'd contracted in his youth. The disease was known as consumption then, for the way it literally consumed and exhausted a person's reservoir of life. One in seven Europeans died of it; one in three of the productive, working, middle-aged. The disease was felt by many to be hereditary. Twenty years after Thoreau's death, Koch proved that it was not.

Using a brand new staining technique and state-of-the-art microscope, Koch identified the rod-shaped causative agent, which he named *Mycobacterium tuberculosis*. It would be some time before an effective treatment existed, but Koch's discovery was critical in paving the way.

Imagine Thoreau living a mere twenty years longer. Time stretches its arms for him. The news of Koch's discovery spread in its day like wildfire; he most certainly would have known of it. How would he have felt then of the "insignificant things" seen under the microscope? What would he have done?

For a man of nature and the natural world, where there was nothing that didn't spark his interest and curiosity, and little that he didn't document scrupulously, year after year, to the tune of 3,000 journal pages, plus correspondence and notes, Thoreau was remarkably reticent when it came to his own health or lack thereof. He rarely mentions it, and never at length, not the length you'd expect of a man of science. Human health and disease had as much to teach him about the laws of nature—about balance, nourishment, depletion, vitality, regeneration, and decay—as did the woods he so loved, and the meadows and streams, but it's as if he were deaf to them.

Or mostly deaf. He does refer to his health from time to time, typically in brief and glancing terms:

"No doubt the healthiest man in the world is prevented from doing what he would like by sickness." (December 21, 1855, in his *Journal*)

"I am inclined to think of late that as much depends on the state of the bowels as of the stars." (December 12, 1859, in his *Journal*)

"I took a severe cold about the 3rd of December, which at length resulted in a kind of bronchitis, so that I have been confined to the house ever since." (letter to an acquaintance dated March 22, 1861)

"I have been sick so long that I have almost forgotten what it is to be well; and yet I feel that it is in all respects only my envelope." (August 15, 1861, letter to Daniel Ricketson)

Many people are private when it comes to their health. They prefer not to prate about their woes and parade their infirmities. Still. From a man devoted—no, obsessively devoted—to the closely observed life, this is precious little.

We never read, for example, how the distance he was able to walk diminished steadily as consumption destroyed his lungs. We never read how tired he was, neither in days able to work a week, nor in hours per day (we know in his last year or two, he stopped doing "original" work and devoted himself to collecting and compiling his writings, which, while not rote or automatic, was a more defined pursuit, like tidying up a tool box or a storeroom, and therefore less tiring . . . a common, if begrudging, accommodation to reality made by the dying). He never counted the number of days he was feverish, and for how long, and when this was accompanied by a shaking chill and drenching sweat. He never talked about how it felt to cough his guts out, and when he wasn't coughing, how it felt to be starved for air, how, beyond being continually short of breath, he was starved for energy, including and most killingly, the energy to form coherent, original thought. He never mentioned, in scientific terms or other-wise, how it felt to have his life eaten away, to be consumed, parasit-ized as it were, from the inside out. How it called to mind a particular parasitic wasp, which itself called to mind a historic, perhaps mythic, event, which he'd read in Virgil, or Ovid. He never talked about any of this, not the fevers, not the wasting, not the breathlessness, not the fact that his own sister Helen died of the same disease at the age of thirty-six.

Suddenly we see a man renowned for being fearlessly outspoken in a different light. Restrained. Discreet. A New Englander, where these qualities are as bred in the bone among the educated and genteel as they are wondered at, and found to be of little use, by those of a more uninhibited, bursting-at-the-seams, confessional nature, such as Walt Whitman, who knew Thoreau and in so many other respects was like him.

It's no sin to be restrained. It's no sin to be discreet. In the right hands, at the right time, these can be virtues, if not gifts.

Which is to say that self-exposure, particularly of the most intimate, gruesome, physical details of one's own body and health, as riveting and irresistible as it may sound, is not everyone's cup of tea.

– 2 –

Today I had tears in my eyes. The feeling hits me every so often out of no-where. What triggered it today? Walking alone in the cold winter morning from the hospital, where I had my pre-op blood draw, to the clinic where I'll have my pre-op physical. The alone part. We all are, but still. It was cold, and I was lonely. (January 15, 2013)

Sitting in exam room, where I've spent thousands upon thousands of hours as MD. Comfortable, familiar. One of Netter's fine illustrations on the wall, this one of the cardiac anatomy. Drawing of heart transected in transverse and coronal planes. Normally I love this stuff, and I love it now. But thinking about getting cut up myself, it also gives me the creeps.

It started so innocently, with this funny little sound. Like tiny bubbles popping on the surface of a liquid. I heard it only when I lay down in bed at night, and only when I exhaled. And not actually with exhalation but afterwards, a little bonus sound. It was funny to hear and kind of cute, like something was down there hiding, a gremlin or something. My wife and I joked and laughed about it. We did this every night for a couple of weeks, until eventually she told me to stop because it was creeping her out. Being a doctor, I felt differently. I was interested and tried to find an explanation. It took a few weeks, and eventually I did. (January 15)

CT scan today. Afterwards, finagle my way into the reading room. Meet the radiologist. Like me, loves his job. More than happy to talk about the study. Doctor to doctor, no holds barred, just the facts. I love it.

My first reaction on seeing the mass: how beautiful. It grows along the path of the lung, and the lung is beautiful. It's a tree, literally, a tree of breath, which means it's the tree of life. All nature is beautiful. (January 3)

After the PET scan, track down the nuclear med doc. He's diligent and careful, which means he has to comment on every little blip he sees, but basically the news is good: the mass is confined to the lung and hasn't spread. I get a shock, though, when he hands me a print-out of the report. It begins: "64 y/o male with mass in . . ."

For years I've read these reports and seen patients described just this way. It's how I describe them myself when I order the tests. "A 64 y/o man. A 61 y/o woman. A 66 . . . 67 . . . 69 y/o." And I think, "That's an old person. Not ancient, but getting on."

The shock is seeing me described this way. It's not the anonymity (though there's plenty of that when you've got cancer, and more to come). It's that I'm not 64, damn it. I'm young. (January 6)

This ability I have. That most doctors have. To view things with a detached, clinical eye. Difficult things, like pain, suffering and illness. To keep them at a distance. Hilary Mantel, in her novel Wolf Hall *has this to say: "There are some strange cold people in this world. It is priests, I think. . . . Training themselves out of natural feeling. They mean it for the best, of course."*

There are some strange cold people in the world. But do not mistake distance for coldness. Some of us use distance because we run too hot, because without it our feelings would overwhelm us.

And yes, it does require training. Any craft, to be of use, requires discipline. Discipline is what allows me the great pleasure of having a candid conversation with my surgeon, when we discuss, basically, how he's going to stab me in the chest and tear my lung out. We could be two generals on the eve of battle, calmly finalizing a take-no-prisoners plan of attack. (January 14)

Spirits good. Try not to think of sharp, pointed objects puncturing my chest. Instead, think of pressing the button of the patient-controlled, post-op dilaudid drip. Swimming in a sea of narcotics. Am very curious about this. (January 16, two days before surgery)

Lots of hugs from my wife. The sweetness just overflows. I feel like I'm living in a state of grace.

Long conversation with my daughter. Like me a literal, concrete thinker. Couldn't quite visualize what the surgery entails, and needed to. So I pulled out my old anatomy textbook. Big, thick book with beautiful, detailed drawings. The one of the lung particularly good. Each lobe clearly marked and color-coded. The surgery textbook also useful.

Explaining is a way of containing. She's of the opinion that, ultimately, we have no control over our fate. Ultimately, I'd have to agree, but short of ultimately, I'd say my fate is in the hands of the man who's going to cut me open.

More tears, after a call from my sister. We say the things we usually don't say. Why the tears? Because the feelings of love and attachment are so old and primitive and sacred that it seems as if we're breaking an oath to speak of them. An unspoken oath between sister and brother, forgotten over the years of living our separate lives, not to desert one another. To be there through thick and thin. And now, if I die in surgery (unlikely), the sacred oath will be broken. (January 17, the day before surgery)

Chest tubes in. Three of them, dangling down like extra appendages. Tube in penis. Tubes in arms. Tubes everywhere, except in nose, now out. Small apical pneumo detected on CXR. Probably asympto. (January 21, post-op day 3)

I've been philosophic, by which I mean:

    a) Take each day as it comes

    b) Don't think too far ahead

    c) Accept what happens and move forward

    d) Don't freak out

    e) Don't get depressed

    f) Maintain curiosity (January 23)

You'd think every moment would be precious. If cancer is good for anything, and I'm not saying it ain't, you'd think it would be good for this. Here's an incomplete list of the good:

1. I've seen and talked to lots of friends. Some I would have in the normal course of events. Others I might not have seen for a year or more.

2. I've learned how a lung is taken out. It's a marvel of science, combining careful attention to detail, deftness and brute force. (As so much of surgery does.) Read a journal report about hand size and surgical outcomes. Data suggest that smaller hand-sized surgeons, by and large females, have better results in a number of procedures. Small hands, one, can slip through much smaller incisions, and two, are more agile and efficient in confined spaces.

3. I've learned this about myself: that I'm not afraid of death in the way I thought I might be. That if I do die from this, I won't kick and curse. I'll be at peace for what I've accomplished.

Will I be at peace for who I've been, which is different? I can't answer that yet. Maybe that's another good from cancer: I can work on this.

4. My son got a haircut.

This requires a brief explanation. How is this good, since hair length, personally, has never been an issue for me? It's good because: one, he's looking for a job, and personal appearance and grooming are important; two, he has a scalp condition that long hair makes infinitely worse; three, in his world, a very special place, there is nothing more difficult or threatening than change of any sort, small or large, miniscule or mighty: they are all the same to him. So even when he knows he should cut his hair, when he has every reason in the world to cut it, he'll avoid cutting it, as he has for years. Out of fear, resistance, inertia, embarrassment. But he did cut it, because I asked him to. Not directly but persuasively. I played the post-op, lying-in-bed, having-him-visit-me-in-the-ICU card. What I'd like most to see when I open my eyes.

Do something good for yourself, I told him, do something good for me.

He cut it himself with an electric clipper. Did an excellent job. Proud, happy to have it shorn, happy at how easy it is to take care of, happy at how his scalp is already starting to heal, happy with how he looks.

So much happiness. Having cancer is almost worth it. (January 23)

My wife this morning says, on a different topic entirely, it's good to take action, even if it's a small action. I heartily agree.

Taking action seems tantamount to being alive.

Making a decision and following it through is one form of action.

Relinquishing control, surrendering to what may be, is another. (January 24)

My surgeon called yesterday with the pathology results. Good news and bad news. The good news: the lymph nodes are clear. The bad: the cancer is bigger than originally thought. Also, there are 'micro-foci of cancer' at the staple line (where the lung was cut out). Meaning there isn't a clear margin between cancer and normal tissue. Meaning it's likely there's cancer still inside. (February 1)

These selections are from a journal I kept after being diagnosed with lung cancer. The journal runs to many thousands of words. Strangely, missing entirely from it is an extraordinary encounter I had after my first surgery with a pulmonary pathologist at the university where I worked, a young, energetic, widely respected expert in the field of lung cancer. Extraordinary for how generous he was, how quick to say yes when I asked if he'd look at my slides and offer his opinion. Extraordinary for how small his office was, despite his standing, how cluttered with books and journals and specimen slides (a hundred years earlier, there would have been jars of pickled, diseased organs and mutant stillborns lining the shelves), how little the clutter mattered to him, and how reassuring this was to me. Extraordinary for how friendly he was, and simultaneously focused on the business at hand, which were the slides I'd brought, which he unpacked and slid into place on the staging platform with practiced agility and grace. Extraordinary for the tingle I felt sitting opposite him and peering into the microscope, a teaching microscope, with two sets of eyepieces. How effortlessly I fell into the role of objective observer and scientist. This stained, two-dimensional slice of the natural world—the beauty of it, the intelligent design of the tissue, the multiplicity of forms, the efficiency—made my heart race. I was catapulted back forty years to my days as a medical student, looking at slides under the microscope, slides of normal tissue, abnormal tissue, normal and abnormal cells, slides of injury, inflammation and repair, slides of disease. In those days there were two main obstacles to a long, happy, prosperous life—at least a long life—cancer and heart disease. The heart could be treated; cancer, not so much. Both were enemies, but cancer was *the* enemy, and the worst possible kind of enemy: evil, irrational, implacable, and inhuman, an alien presence to wake our worst nightmares and most deep-seated fears.

Under the microscope a cancer cell looks different from a normal cell: its nucleus is dark and fat, effacing all but the thinnest rim of normalcy. A dark fat evil eye, sinister and malignant. As a student, I'd developed a reflex visceral reaction of horror and antipathy on seeing it. Forty years later, I felt it again—my stomach clenched, the breath caught in my chest—as though it were yesterday.

How extraordinary, I thought, the persistence of reflexive behavior. How extraordinary, the strength of the xenophobic response. And how extraordinarily quickly these dissipated, as the scientist in me, the lover of knowledge and of nature, took over, and shock and fear gave way to awe and wonder. I understood what I hadn't forty years before, what no one had: cancer is not alien. It's not other. It's our own cells gone awry, and as such, it's a window into who we are, a deep deep window into the infinitely complex, infinitely precise, exquisitely balanced, bacchanal of life. Cancer teaches us how cells divide and what makes them stop dividing (or in cancer's case, not). How one cell, sperm and egg, becomes trillions of cells. How cells differentiate into other cells. How from a single lumpy homogenous-ish mass we sprout fingers, brains, and blood. It teaches us how we grow, and in nature growth is life.

Having cancer is no picnic, but thinking about cancer, for a thinker, is about as good as it gets. Its dark, fat eye may presage nasty things to come, but it isn't evil. It's beautiful. Miraculous even, the way all life is. It signifies imbalance, which is a fact of life, and at the same time holds the keys to restoring the balance. The keys, in effect, to its own demise.

All at once, I felt a lightening of the spirit. In place of dread, I was filled with a sense of wonder and respect. And gratitude: toward the doctor for his help and expertise, for being my Virgil; and for being a doctor myself, with the kind of mind—some would say, split personality—that is drawn to the ghastly and unusual as a moth to a flame. All doctors feel this to some degree. It's not insensitivity; it's the love of solving puzzles. For a doctor, morbid curiosity is oxymoronic.

A month later, hoping to get rid of whatever cancer remained inside, I had a second lobe of my lung removed. I was now missing two out of five. That's a lot to be missing. On the upside, I still had three left.

Oncologists are nothing if not optimists, and mine assured me I could run a marathon on three lobes. Our mountain expedition was no marathon, not as mountain expeditions go, but for some of us, including me, it was no cakewalk either.

I was there to honor Thoreau, but more than that I was there to see if I could climb a mountain again, and to be with my friends who climbed mountains, to share in that particular joy, which, as I've tried to explain, is profound and endorphin-rich. Where the air is thin the pleasure is commensurably fat: somewhere there's an equation that describes this.

At 10,000 feet the effective oxygen percentage is roughly two-thirds what it is at sea level. The summit of Peak 12,691 was over 12,000 feet (12,707 to be precise), where it would be measurably less. I was already down by nearly 40 percent. Here's the equation I was working with:

On one side: thinness of air + absence of lung + long layoff + no shame in a crippled man's failing.

On the other side: the feeling of wild, disinhibited freedom and exultation of spirit on being above tree line in a land of giants. And while no shame in failing, no joy in it either. I wanted to prove to myself I could do it.

An unbalanced equation from the start, heavily weighted toward reaching the summit.

Long story short, I did. I made it to the top, along with ten others. The day before summiting, our band camped at one of the Wonder Lakes, which could be the name of all alpine lakes, because all are sublime, unique, and wonderful. When we arrived, the wind was wonderfully fierce. At one point it lifted the water of the lake as though a cupped hand were scooping it up, then flinging it. We had to hide behind trees and rocks to keep from being blown over. After many hours the gale calmed enough so that we could set up camp, which we did in a little meadow.

In the Sierras, meadows are rarely named. Like the lakes, they could all be named wonderful. No one questioned the wisdom and long-delayed justice in naming a mountain Thoreau, though it would have been more apt, considering the man, to name a meadow. I offer the following by way of rectification:

Let the small grassy hollow a stone's throw from the shore of the lake where we took shelter, slept, and ate, and which was bounded by several large granite boulders, two enormous white pines, and the lake's small outlet creek, hereby be known as Thoreau Meadow. Further, let it be said that, though the meadow was not by any stretch of the imagination big, just enough to accommodate our six or seven tents, bigness, as Thoreau well knew, is of the mind. The dimensions of consciousness exist in a different universe than those of physical space.

He was big in thought, and big in championing the value of thought, and the value of self-sufficiency. As a writer, he understood the importance of silence and solitude. Which is not to say he was immune to the pleasures of company or the need for acknowledgment and recognition. The need is a feature of all living things, without which there would be no future living things. The need to recognize, and be recognized, is the first step toward coming together with others of one's own kind, of bonding, perhaps physically, perhaps not, with one, or with many, in a couple or a group. Recognition begins with the process of display, of identifying oneself by means of color, shape, size, body language, facial expression, sound, scent, heat, vibration, spoken or written word, and of simultaneously, or almost simultaneously, identifying others. This is true at every level of life: microscopic life, macroscopic life, cells, bacteria, ants, and humans.

Thoreau famously wrote about ants, for whom being recognized—friend or foe—is a matter of survival. For Thoreau the writer, recognition helped feed the ego, which all writers need. It helped pay the bills. Beyond that, it helped satisfy his need to be heard. Like any writer, he wanted an audience. He certainly preferred having one to having none. Though being a writer, he understood there was only one audience member, in the end, worth listening to.

Hard to say how he'd react to having a mountain named after him. Tempting to think he'd brush if off as superficial and unnecessary; that a thing was a thing, with all its essential and fundamental thingness, without having a name attached to it. At one point he writes as much, that a name runs the danger of diminishing the thing being named. At other times he writes just the opposite, often with vehemence.

But it's done. Peak 12,691 is no longer merely a number. I for one am happy to have a Mt. Thoreau. Our modest expedition got me to read him again. It got me among friends and kindred spirits. It got me up, then down, the mountain, to the party afterwards, which was magical and boisterous, and lasted two days.

All this happened a year and a half ago, though today, as I write, it seems like yesterday. Since the cancer, time has been a consistently inconsistent companion, expanding and contracting as if it could. Days fly by. Nights, not infrequently, stretch on. More of both lately, since learning that the cancer's back. Not in a single lobe this time, but all over.

***

Thoreau was as reticent in talking about his impending death as he was in talking about what led to it. When he did, you have to admire his humor and wit. In answer to the question "Have you made your peace with God?" he replied, "I did not know we had ever quarreled." And to a friend who was pestering him for a glimpse, a word, of what lay on "the opposite shore," he replied, "one world at a time."

He hardly talked at all about the literal process of dying itself. These days, with advanced directives, decisions about end-of-life care, and support groups everywhere you look, where nothing is off limits, it's hard *not* to.

In my experience, there are, roughly speaking, two ways to go: fast and slow. There is something to be said for sudden death: whatever suffering is to be had lasts, at most, a few seconds. Presumably. After that, peace. Presumably. No one really knows.

Not so much peace for everyone else. To the living, sudden death shatters the peace. It's like a body blow, but to the psyche. For some, the aftershock lasts years.

In slow death you get the shock first, when you get the news: cancer, metastatic. Treatable but not curable, and maybe not even treatable. Now, for however long you have, you do your best to get the most out of life, to enjoy yourself and be as decent and good and as true to yourself, and loving of others, and of life in general, as possible. Be prepared to be surprised: at times I've been so happy that I scarcely recognize myself.

The value of a slow death lies in the opportunity to shed your skin and reinvent yourself, if needed. Or to stick to your guns, if not. In either case, it's a good time to turn your lens on what's important, and to sharpen the focus.

Six weeks before his death Thoreau wrote this: "I *suppose* that I have not many months to live; but, of course, I know nothing about it. I may add that I am enjoying existence as much as ever, and regret nothing."

Today I got up early, intending to begin the difficult process of sorting through a lifetime's worth of possessions, giving and throwing away as much as I could, lightening the load for my wife and kids. I filled up about half a box with books, when the sun, which was not quite up, hit the big puffy springtime clouds suspended above the Berkeley hills, which I could see out my window, setting them aglow, then ablaze, with gold and poppy-colored light. I had to stop and sit down. What I was seeing and feeling was too astonishing and spectacular to let pass unremarked.

After the sun had risen and the show was over, I found myself thinking about death. Not being dead, but the act of dying, the physical sensations I'd have, and the mental, the cognitive, experience during the last moments, the final transition between life and death. "How interesting will *that* be?" I thought.

I shared this thought with my wife.

"You're curious," she said. It wasn't a question.

I answered anyway. "Of course."

Fidelity

I. Born Torn

Lydell called me with the news that he was torn. This, of course, was no news at all. Lydell has been torn since birth. This time it had to do with his sons, Max and Ernest. The boys were twins, and still in utero. Lydell couldn't decide whether to have them circumcised or not.

He'd done the legwork. When it came to so deeply personal a matter, he was nothing if not thorough. Uncircumcised men, he had found, did have a slightly higher incidence of infection, but the infections were usually trivial and easily treated. Balanitis, where the foreskin became red and inflamed, was uncommon. Phimosis, where the inflammation led to scarring, trapping the penis in its hood and making erections and intercourse painful (if not impossible), was likewise rare.

Circumcision, by contrast, was a uniformly traumatic event. What effect this trauma had was debatable, although the preponderance of evidence suggested long-lasting and not entirely beneficial sequelae. After all, such a grisly and disfiguring procedure at so young and tender an age. At any age. Was this absolutely necessary for a man to be a man? Some thought not.

As to the issue of pleasure, there seemed little question. The greater the amount of intact skin, the greater the concentration of nerves. The greater the concentration of nerves, the better the sensation. And while sensation itself did not guarantee pleasure, there was certainly the chance that it might.

On the other hand was tradition. Lydell was a Jew. Jews were circumcised. Judith, his wife, thought the boys might think it slightly odd if they were not. But she could see the other side, too, most notably the avoidance of unnecessary pain and trauma. If pressed, she would probably have cast her vote with letting the poor things' tiny penises be, but in the end, she deferred to her husband, who not only had a penis but strong views as to its proper handling and use.

Lydell consulted a rabbi, who advised him to search his soul. He suggested he remember his parentage and lineage, and if he still had doubts after that, to take a good hard look in the mirror. In addition, he referred him to the Old Testament, First Kings, Chapter 3, which spoke of King Solomon, the great and illustrious Jewish leader, who, when faced with two women, each claiming to be the mother of the same infant, advised them to share the baby by cutting it in two. The false mother agreed, the true one did not, and thus was the question of motherhood decided.

Lydell pondered the well-known tale. On the face of it, the message seemed clear enough: be clever, be insightful, value life (and love) above possessions. But the lesson seemed difficult to generalize, and Lydell sensed a deeper meaning that was far from transparent. He puzzled it day and night, up until the very hour of the boys' birth.

They came out strapping and healthy, with dark, curly hair, brown eyes, and flattened little baby faces. Identical faces, at that. Identical bodies. They were, in fact, identical twins.

It was a transformative event for Lydell. Both the birth and the fact that they were identical. A light seemed to shine from above (it was a sunny day). Suddenly, the path was clear. Ernest and Max, Max and Ernest: the very sameness of the children held the key to the solution. An individual was a precious thing—perhaps the most precious thing in the world. Just as the true mother would not permit her only child to be split asunder, so Lydell would not allow his two sons to grow up indistinguishable from one another. They were unique, and thus would be uniquely set apart.

One would be circumcised (this fell to Max). The other (Ernest) would not.

Judith took issue with this, strong issue, but Lydell would not be moved. He was resolute, and she had little choice but go along. She soothed herself (or tried) with the belief that somehow, somewhere, he knew best. The penis was his territory: she kept telling herself this. It was her mantra during this difficult and trying time. The penis was his.

II. Poolside, Where a Stone Tossed Years Before Creates a Ripple

He had a lingering medical problem. She had a difficult marriage. They met at the pool where their children were taking swimming lessons.

Her eyes were large and compassionate.

His hair was to his shoulders.

He wore a silver bracelet and held his wrist coquettishly.

She favored skirts that brushed the floor.

They sat on a wooden bench with their backs to the wall, watching the children swim. They spoke without turning, like spies. Pointed observations delivered in a glancing, offhanded way.

She was a devoted mother.

He was a solicitous father.

He had a daughter. She, two sons.

The swimming lessons lasted thirty minutes. To him this was never quite enough. He worked alone and felt the need for contact. He wanted more.

She was often distracted by her sons, delighted by their antics and their progress. She would clap for them and call out her encouragement.

He sensed in some small way that she was using them as a buffer, or a baffle, to deflect his interest in her and hers in him, to disrupt their fledgling chemistry.

They spoke about their jobs. About their children's schools. About religion. She was Jewish. They spoke about the Holocaust. She decried the lingering hatred. It upset her, even as she understood it. She was interested, in theory, in forgiveness and reconciliation.

He listened to her closely and attentively, often nodding his agreement. He showed his sympathy and understanding, smelled her hormones, won her trust.

At the end of the lessons they parted without ceremony, sometimes without so much as a word. She wrapped her sons in towels and escorted them to the dressing room, waiting outside the door until they were done. He did the same for his daughter. Afterwards, there was candy and then the walk to the car. Often the five of them walked together, though they rarely talked. The kids weren't interested, and the grown-ups had had their time together. Half an hour, session done.

III. Brain Work

His name was Wade. He'd been married twenty years. There was a family history of mental illness, notably depression (a grandmother) and manic-depression (a great aunt). Another grandmother suffered from feelings of inferiority. Wade's father had a number of compulsions, none incapacitating, while his mother, heroic in so many ways, lived with the anxieties and minor hysterias typical of a woman of thwarted ambition with too much time on her hands.

Wade himself, like his great aunt, was a victim of mood swings. A year previously, after a brief bout of mania followed by a much longer one of despair, he started taking medication.

It was a good year for medication. Sales were booming, and three of the top ten drugs on the market were specifically designed to treat disturbances of mood. This represented an enormous advance from the days of his great aunt, who had to make do with electric shock (it served her well), insulin shock (not so well), and prolonged hospitalizations.

Wade tried Prozac, but it left him feeling muzzy-headed, about as animated as a stone. He tried Zoloft, with the same effect. Paxil likewise left him feeling like a zombie, and in addition, it robbed him of his sex drive.

He was too young to go without sex. At forty-six, he felt he was still too young to be a zombie. So he stopped the medication.

Eli Lilly called him. Pfizer called him. SmithKline Beecham called him, too. They sympathized with his problem. Sacrifice was difficult. No man should have to give up his manhood. But likewise, no man, particularly no American man, should have to be depressed.

Ironically, after stopping the pills, he got better. He was no longer victimized by sudden bouts of mania, nor was he paralyzed by depression. He was able to work, to care for his daughter and be a decent husband to his wife. He was sane again, and functional, in all ways except one. He remained impotent.

This happens, said his doctor. Give it time. This happens, said Lilly, Pfizer, and Beecham. Read the small print. We regret the inconvenience. We're working on a cure.

Months went by, and he didn't recover. His penis didn't get hard, not even in the morning when his bladder was full. His penis, poor thing, rarely stirred.

IV. Virtue and Necessity

Judith had no intention of having an affair. She believed in the sanctity of marriage, most especially her own. That said, her husband had of late been going through one of those times of his. One of those intense and trying times of self-intoxication, when he couldn't see beyond himself, couldn't think or talk about anything but *his* desires, *his* beliefs, *his* needs.

Judith did her best to show compassion, but in truth, she was tired of his histrionics. Ten years of marriage, eight since the boys were born, had taken their toll. She wanted a man, not another child to care for.

Men were useful, or they could be . . . and lovable, that too—vaguely, she remembered this. They had that male way about them, that male sense of entitlement and privilege, that male look and feel. In theory, there was much to recommend a man. They were sexy. They smelled good. They got things done.

She wanted one of those.

V. In Heat

The pool was by the ocean. Cypress trees and sand dunes ringed the parking lot. Across the street in one direction was a golf course. In another was the city zoo.

Often, when walking to their cars, they'd hear a high-pitched keening sound. A peacock's cry, perhaps an animal in heat. Or a golfer in extremis.

She was a businesswoman. She organized trade conventions.

He was a cartoonist. He made his living with ink and pen.

He had a fey and predatory nature.

She had a sixth sense.

Their conversations were never casual.

She was in a book group, all women. Why all women? he asked, to get her talking about her womanhood. To feel the heart and soul of women.

It's safer, she said. The whole sexual thing. And women have a way of talking. They have an understanding.

They see beneath the surface.

They share the same complaints.

What complaints? he asked.

She smiled. So many.

For three months they met. They never touched, not once. Sat an inch apart, backs to the wall, sweaty and sticky in the steamy equatorial heat of the pool. The children were their safety net. The children and their marriages, their loyalties, their loves, their pacts.

VI. Setting the Record Straight

I'd like to clear my chest. Bear with me on this. I've known several Judiths in my life. One was a belly dancer. Another was a lawyer. The one who stands out the most was a redheaded woman, big boned and brassy, out of Nebraska. Married a man name of Chan, Sam Chan, an acupuncturist. The two of them emigrated to Argentina, where they set up practice. As far as I know, none of these Judiths ever worked on conventions, or for that matter, had twins. But it's possible. I just can't say for sure.

As for Lydell, the only Lydell I remember with certainty was a football player, and I may be wrong about that. It might have been basketball, and come to think of it, the name was Lyell, not Lydell.

On the other hand, this guy Wade, this is a guy I know. And I have to say, my opinion of him is not high. I met him at the pool—Judith introduced us—and we ended up seeing each other a few times on the side. So what I know about him is firsthand information. It's gospel. Same goes for his wife, a helluva nice lady name of Flora, whom I also had the chance to meet. What she sees in a guy like this is beyond me. The man's a charmer, no question, especially with the ladies. But the fact is, he only delivers what he himself decides to. What and when. That's the type of guy he is. A manipulator.

His whole purpose in coming on to Judith was to save his marriage. That's how he justified it. It was the impotence thing—he just couldn't stand not being able to get a hard-on. It was a humiliation to him, he told me. A humiliation and a disgrace.

He and Flora had tried everything. The pills, the pumps, the injections, the talk. He'd been to a prostitute. And hypnotism, he'd tried that. Now he was trying a married woman.

He didn't plan to take it all the way, even if she wanted to. He had his limits, or so he said. It was the idea of it, the titillation. The journey, not the destination. The hunt.

It was a noble purpose, I suppose. To save a marriage. (Although to hear Flora tell it, she was getting by all right. She was, by nature, independent, and had her work to occupy her. She also kept a plastic dildo in her bedside table to use whenever.)

A noble purpose, but ignobly executed. The man was using Judith. That's what I can't stomach.

Then again, she was using him.

VII. A Somewhat Tortured Logic

The boys had a pet rat named Snowflake. She was a gentle, friendly rat, with a white coat and a long pink tail. At the age of a year

Snowflake developed a tumor in her side. It was small at first, the size of a grape, but it grew rapidly. By six months it was the size and consistency of a ripe plum. They took her to a vet, who diagnosed a lipoma, in other words, a big ball of fat. This was good news in the sense that it wasn't cancer. Less good was the two-hundred-dollar fee to have it excised.

Lydell felt the surgery unwarranted. Snowflake was a rat, and rats could be had for pennies. Beyond the issue of cost was the deeper question of value, the life lesson about man and the natural world. In Lydell's view, intervention was far too often man's way with nature. And it didn't have to be. There was much to be said for watchfulness, for letting the world weave its intricate and beautiful web without disrupting its threads prematurely, if ever.

There was also the issue of anthropocentrism. Judging the rat unhappy in its current condition was so quintessentially human a gesture, so human an assumption, that it could easily be a mistake. Perhaps, the creature was content with its burden. Perhaps, it didn't care.

The question of consciousness came up: did the rat notice that it was different from other rats? Was it even aware of the mass?

After some discussion, it was agreed that the rat did, in fact, notice. There was really no ignoring a lump that size. But whether it cared, whether its level of consciousness included a sense of dissatisfaction with the ways things were and a desire to change them—this was uncertain. Snowflake had such a genial temperament to begin with. Even when the mass, after being dragged along the floor of the cage for months on end, became infected, her demeanor didn't noticeably change. Perhaps she slowed down a bit, but then she had never been much interested in speed. And being a rat of good breeding and character, qualities the boys learned about in detail, she wasn't the type to complain.

The tumor grew. At a subsequent visit the vet was frankly amazed. "This animal should have been dead months ago," he exclaimed, a comment notable, if not for its thoughtlessness, then certainly for its ambiguity. The boys were left to ponder just what exactly he meant.

Max, a confident, outspoken child, assumed he meant that without the operation Snowflake would be better off dead. He didn't want her to die, and he argued with his father to intervene. He invoked the rights of animals, the concept of *tzedakah* (charitable deeds, from a charitable heart), the universality of souls. A canny, verbally precocious boy, he presented his case eloquently (albeit unsuccessfully). In this he made his father proud.

Ernest was, by nature, more reserved. He was slow to express his opinions and whenever possible avoided conflict. This had earned him a reputation, right or wrong, for being shy.

On the surface he accepted his father's decision. The rat would live its life, then die. But underneath the surface he knew otherwise. Underneath, his mind was rife with dreams and fantasies of a different sort. If Snowflake should have been dead but wasn't, then clearly she had powers hitherto unimagined. He'd read about such beings—entities, they were called—in comic books; he'd seen them on TV. Alien entities. Invincible, ineffable, and immortal.

Snowflake was no ordinary rat. Each day she lived and beat the odds was proof of this. She was something different. Something special. Something more.

Ernest therefore didn't worry. Whatever happened, Snowflake would be okay. Consequently, there was no need to argue with his father. On the contrary, he agreed with him. Leave the rat alone.

Judith, meanwhile, fumed.

She agreed that a rat was a rat, but this particular rat, their rat, was a pet. Pets were family, and family needed to be looked after. She thought what Lydell was doing, what he was teaching, was stingy, gratuitous, and cruel.

And insufferable. And sadistic. And Nazi-Darwinistic (she got to him with that). And, quite frankly, obscene.

He got her back one night. Got her bad. He was talking about the money they were saving by letting nature take its course. Then he dropped the bomb.

He wanted to use it to get Ernest circumcised.

Ernest at this point was eight.

Judith said, No way.

Lydell pleaded his point. He admitted to having made a mistake.

Live with it, she said.

He couldn't. —I look at him and think, how can this be a Jew?

—He's a Jew if he wants to be. If you let him.

—I'm ashamed of myself. I set him apart. I thought I knew best, but I didn't.

—You want to atone? Leave him alone. Practice what you preach.

—Let's ask him, said Lydell.

Her eyes flashed. —Don't you dare.

VIII. Idealism! Temptation! Restraint!

She had long fingers, hazelnut eyes, and a passion for people.

He had a soft mouth and a way with words.

She missed the freedom and excitement of her younger days.

He dressed for the occasions. Wore his brightest colors. Worked for her attention.

She saw in him a respite. A way station on the arduous and life-long path of marriage. She was going through a period of reflection, a taking account of her life. She was recalling what had been put aside, what dream of self, what vision. Retracing her past to its fork points: the choice to marry, to have a career, to be a mother. And prior to that, the choice to end the wildness and anarchy of a protracted adolescence, the choice to grow up and follow the rules. To be a solid citizen. To practice self-respect and love.

Which she intended to continue.

Being an honorable woman. With honorable desires.

She never littered. She never spat. She wouldn't cheat.

A woman of conviction. But human.

He was a nontraditional cartoonist. He favored irregularly shaped panels as opposed to the traditional squares. The wilder and more improbable the better. He liked to experiment with sequencing, as well. Linear cartooning was too constrained for his taste. Too contrived. If he was going to the trouble of drawing all those pictures, he wanted people to look at them, not skim past them as if they were the written word.

He had Ideas. He spoke of a modern aesthetic. Commitment to craft and to Art with a capital A. He was passionate, which made it easier to tolerate his pomposity.

She was drawn to him.

He thrilled at the game they were playing.

He also had qualms.

He meant no harm.

She was flattered by his attention. Interested in his ideas. At one time she herself had painted.

Aha, he chortled. A kindred spirit!

Hardly that, she replied. A hobbyist, at best. But nothing at all since the boys were born. She missed the creativity of it, the tactile pleasure of brush in hand, the fun. Not that she couldn't live without. Obviously, she could. And furthermore, she didn't believe in regrets.

He agreed. Regrets were useless.

Yes, she said. Completely useless.

Utterly, he added with panache.

At that they ceased to speak, meditating silently on the uselessness of regret.

They were so determined to be friends, and not lovers. To rise above their mutual attraction. This was their goal, which they spoke of in gestures, if not words. Friendship was the Holy Grail of a male-female relationship. The Ultimate Prize. They would prove it could be done.

Mirabile dictu! Such lofty ideals! Such audacity. Intimacy without jeopardy. Freedom of expression without chaos. Pleasure without pain.

IX. Further Revelations

How do I know these things? Word gets around. These are my friends.

If you believe Wade, what he was doing was for a good cause. If you ask me, Flora let him get away with too much. But she saw it differently. She, after all, had to live with his mood swings, and he'd been free of them for nearly a year. She wasn't about to upset that particular apple cart. Her philosophy was fairly straightforward: if a man wanted to hang himself, so be it. The tighter the leash, the greater the chance it would break.

Judith, quite simply, was filling a need. When you're with someone like Lydell for as long as she was, someone with his capacity for self-absorption, you can't help but have periods of loneliness and longing. Periods when you feel yourself shriveling for lack of companionship. Periods of self-doubt when you wonder if anyone hears or sees you at all.

Judith fought these feelings. She had work, which helped. She had her children. And now she had a new companion, someone who wanted her around, someone who looked at her and listened.

It was a flirtation of ideas, she told herself. A flirtation of interests. A flirtation of spirit and, therefore, of necessity.

Flirtation, she felt, did not preclude fidelity. On the contrary. Fidelity depended on respect, and it was self-respect that made her flirt. God, she knew, helped those who helped themselves. It was up to her to make her presence known.

X. The Scholar Finds a Way

Sabbath Day. Lydell wears a yarmulke pinned to his head and a many-fringed tallit around his hefty shoulders. In his anguish and his fervor he has turned to the Bible. The Book of First Samuel, Chapter 18, wherein David slays two hundred Philistine men and brings their fore-skins to King Saul (who had only requested a hundred) as dowry for his daughter Michal's hand in marriage. What King Saul wants with so many foreskins, what he does with them, is not mentioned. Lydell can only speculate. Reading the Holy Scriptures has him in a barbaric, morbidly Old Testament mood.

King Saul might have made a tapestry of them, sewn together with the finest threads.

Or a flag, a battle standard to be borne against the heathen armies.

A patchwork quilt.

A bridal veil.

A blanket for his wives.

While fresh, he could have used them as grafts for poorly healing wounds.

Once dried, as snack food for the troops, like pemmican.

Or party favors.

Or rewards for jobs well done.

Yahweh, God in Heaven, God of Lydell's father and his father's father, is an angry God. He is a spiteful God, a savage God, a vengeful God. But He is a smart and clever God, too.

Lydell has one more thought. One that King Solomon, son of David and grandson of Saul, might have approved of. Solomon with whom he feels kinship, Solomon the wise and understanding, Solomon the just. Solomon who in his later years forsook his religion for that of his wives. Solomon who, smitten with love, turned from Judaism to the pagan faith.

A foreskin can be reattached. Not one cut off in a fly-infested battlefield and carried for days by camel in a rank and grimy sack, but a fresh one, a hygienically removed one, a pretty pink virginal one. There are doctors, cosmetologists, who will do anything for a price. If Lydell can't get his son into the fold, he can join him outside the fold. It would be an act of atonement. A day to remember. A yom kippur.

XI. Visions of Grandeur

He wanted to touch her. He wanted to cup his hand on her beautiful ass and slide it into her crack. Smell her, lick her, slather his body with her tart and liquidy self.

He thrilled at the thought of it, the temptation.

He wondered if this was the mania. If it was, he could wash his hands of responsibility. You couldn't blame a person for being ill.

Besides, he was serving Flora.

Patient, loving, flint-eyed Flora. Faithful Flora, who gave him all the slack he needed to hang himself.

XII. Onan the Barbarian

It was Flora, incidentally, who alerted me to a recent survey of Net users that found ten times as many synonyms for male, as compared to female, masturbation. She was doing research for a book on gender and technology. While not particularly surprised at the disparity, she did find it rather offensive. She was also somewhat dismayed.

Religion, politics, and humor were common themes among the more than two hundred male-oriented entries, although a good number seemed chosen solely on the basis of alliteration or rhyme. As for women, the themes ranged from the pedestrian to the sweepingly grandiose, from the biblical to the sublime. Among the examples: "doing my nails," "parting the Red Sea," "surfing the channel," and "flicking the bean." And, of course, that old metaphysical standby, "nulling the void."

Flora makes a good point. The list, while notable, is decidedly short. Is this because women masturbate less than men? A common belief, but one that is unsupported by the data. Is it because they talk about it less? Again, the data say no. Could it be that they simply refused to participate in the poll?

Or have we been silenced? (We, I say, for I take this quite personally—an injustice to one, male or female, is an injustice to all.) Shamefully silenced, I might add, our lips sewn together by the threads of inequity, our tongues disenfranchised from the very words we would use to express our self-love.

We may not "tease the weasel," we keepers of the flame. (Why on earth would we ever do that?) We may not "tug the slug" or "pump the python." Nor, routinely, do we "bop the bishop" or "make the bald man puke." But listen. We surely burp the baby, we toss the salad, we choke the chicken, we pop the cork, and at least every few weeks we whip up a batch of instant pudding. And yes, oh yes, we do sometimes have sex with someone we love.

We've been silenced, I say! Robbed of speech (if not thought), cheated in all the ways we have always been cheated.

Tickling the taco. Brushing the beaver. Making soup. Rolling the dough.

Is this what they think we do all day? Imagine. It's outrageous.

We are more than homebodies. More than domestics. More than mothers and whores.

We need to rise up. The time has come to null the void and give these words a second meaning, a meaning more powerful and self-fulfilling than staying home to surf the channel or idly flick the bean. We can brush the beaver later, ladies. The void needs nulling now.

We need to be creative. On behalf of Flora and everyone else who has ever felt the yoke of inequality, I incite you: soar above your own Mt. Baldy. Be irreverent. Be enticing. Pound the peanut. Pick the peony. Wave to Dr. Kitty. Laugh out loud.

Send your words and phrases, your ditties and your doggerel, your witty little euphemisms and inventions, your unchained melodies to me. Send them quickly. Send them to my web site. Everyone's a poet.

Send them now.

XIII. underwaterworld

The children were diving for hoops. Slapping the water, struggling downward to the bottom of the pool, then splashing to the surface like puppies.

—I'm happy with my choices, she said. All in all.

—I'm happy we met, he replied.

She waved to one of her sons, who had succeeded in getting a ring.

—No? he asked.

—Yes, she said.

—Outside of my wife I've never had an intimate female friend, he said.

She waved to her other son, who was poised on the edge of the pool, building up the nerve to jump.

—You're a beautiful woman.

—Don't, she said.

—I'm only observing.

She fell silent.

He told her not to worry. He was impotent.

This interested her.

He thought it might. Not entirely impotent, he added. Lately, he'd been having signs of life.

She changed the subject.

The book group had been reading Dante. She told him of a dream she had.

—We were pilloried outside the gates of Macy's.

—The gates?

—The gates, the doors. Whatever. You on one side, me on the other.

—People streaming in and out?

—Lots. We were naked.

—How embarrassing.

—Yes. Exceedingly.

—What was our crime?

—Swimming.

—Swimming naked?

—No, just swimming.

—That's it?

—Yes.

—Swimming's no crime.

—It wasn't the swimming, she said. It was the fun.

XIV. The Art of Compromise

Judith had been thinking. Maybe Lydell was right. Not that Ernest should be circumcised, but that he at least should be talked to. Presented with the options. Sounded out.

She spoke to him alone one day after school. He was in his room, playing with his pet. Or rather stroking her fur and comforting her. The tumor was now enormous. The days of the entity known as Snowflake, at least on earth, were clearly numbered.

Ernest, unlike his brother Max, was not a verbal child. He came across as rather distant sometimes. But he never missed a word that was said. He absorbed and processed everything. His mind was as facile as anyone's, and his inner world was deep.

He listened patiently to his mother, and when she finished, surprised her by saying he wanted to have the circumcision done. She asked him why.

—Because, he said.

She pressed him. —Because why?

He hesitated a moment. —Because I deserve it.

It was an ambiguous statement, and one that begged for an explanation. First, however, she reiterated that in her eyes, in everyone's eyes, he was fine—he was perfect—just the way he was.

—I want to be like everybody else, he said.

—The world's a big place. Everybody's different.

—I don't want to be.

Her heart went out to him. —I understand, she said.

He asked if it would hurt. She said it would. He said he didn't want anyone to know.

—Not Max?

He didn't mean Max.

—I'll have to tell your father, she said.

—Let's surprise him, said Ernest.

—I don't think he'd like that.

—It's my choice, isn't that what you said?

—To a point, said his mother.

—It's private, he said. Between you and me. Like between you and that man.

—What man?

Ernest averted his eyes. —You know.

XV. The Sweet Embraceable

You can put yourself in someone else's shoes, you can even get inside their shirt and pants, but it doesn't mean you know them. It's guesswork who they are and what they're thinking and feeling. Guesswork and maybe intuition. As an outsider, you do your level best, but you never really know.

It's what they say and do, not think. If a guy says he's faithful, despite the fact he's getting hard-ons plotting how to get some chick in bed, he's faithful. If a woman says she's faithful, despite the fact she's sitting squarely on the fence, she's faithful.

If they don't touch, they're faithful. If they don't think, they're dead.

The two of them didn't touch. I mentioned that already. Not at the pool or anywhere else. Not once.

Wait a minute. I forgot. They did touch. But only once.

It happened in a neighborhood cafe. They had a date, a nighttime assignation. The kids were tucked at home in bed.

The swimming lessons had been over for several weeks. They'd spoken once by phone but hadn't seen each other. He was carrying a briefcase in one hand. With the other he touched her palm in greeting. Lightly, like a whisper, or a veil. Imperceptibly, she caught her breath. She let the contact linger.

He said, —I've been thinking of you.

She said, —Did you get my letter?

—No, he said.

They took a table in the corner, ordered coffee and dessert.

—I've started to paint again, she said.

—How wonderful, he replied.

—Watercolors. I used to paint with them a lot.

—What made you start again?

—You, she said.

His penis stirred.

—I've given myself two hours a week. Not much, but it's a start.

—A start is all you need.

—I told you in the letter. I'm surprised you didn't get it.

—You could have called, he said.

She had wanted to. But in the wanting knew she shouldn't.

He said, —I've been painting, too. Drawing really. Cartoons. Of us.

Her heart sped up. She felt nervous and excited. "Us" had never been mentioned before. "Us" meant husband and wife.

—I'd like to see them.

He told her they were pornographic. He'd brought them along.

—I think they'll turn you on, he said.

She felt a little flutter in her chest. —Well then, maybe not. Maybe I shouldn't.

—They do me, he added.

He could have said "you," not "they." He had before, or almost.

Then again, he could have brought a carriage drawn by horses. He could have brought a slipper.

She had to smile.

—Do you do drawings of your wife? she asked.

The question gave him pause. —On occasion. Why do you ask?

—Cartoons? Pornographic ones?

He shrugged.

—I don't want anyone getting hurt, she said.

—No one's been hurt, he said. And then, —I don't either.

She wanted to see the pictures. Itched to see them.

Equally, she was determined not to compromise her marriage. Not to act dishonorably. She wondered what behavior this allowed.

She felt torn.

He said, —I'm sorry. I didn't mean to cause you grief.

He said, —I didn't mean to tempt you.

He was wearing silver that night. A silver chain around his neck. A silver earring. A silver bracelet, the same he'd worn the day that they first met.

He had washed his hair in chamomile shampoo. He had used a scented body soap.

He said, —I'm wrong. I have been tempting you.

She felt the truth in this. —Why?

—To see how far you'll go. To test your limits.

—Why?

—Because I don't trust mine.

—And mine you do? She didn't know whether to be flattered or insulted. —You're daring me to be unfaithful? Is that it?

—No, he said. I'm daring you not to be.

How puerile, she thought. How unappealing and crude.

He didn't care for her. She saw this plainly now. Nor did she care for him.

It came as something of a revelation. As did what followed: they cared for each other equally.

How remarkable, she thought. How apposite.

—Show me the pictures, she said.

He took a folder from his briefcase and handed it to her. His penis, which had defervesced, showed signs of life.

She stuffed the folder in her purse. —I'll look at them later.

—They're yours, he said. Keep them. Look at them whenever.

It was the last they were to see of each other. Both knew it.

She wanted to give him something in return.

—A hug, he suggested.

She thought it over. Rising, she pulled on her coat.

—I'll say no to that, she said.

He had risen also, expectantly. Now he felt cheated, and incomplete.

—Take it home, she said.

—Take what home?

—That impulse. That hug. Take it home and give it to your wife.

These were her parting words.

Upon thinking them over, he found, astonishingly, that they were exactly what he wanted to hear.

XVI. The Gift of the Magi

Solomon was wise, but he wasn't all wise. Lydell was crazy, but his motives were pure.

He had the operation. He did it in secret. While he was healing, he dressed and undressed in private. To forestall questions and minimize discomfort, he slept with his back to his wife.

Judith assumed she was being punished for her philandering. Never mind that she had resisted, that she in the end had proved stalwart and faithful. Adultery was as much of the mind as of the body. Her husband might not know the details, but he had doubtlessly suffered. Had the roles been reversed, she would have suffered for sure.

She swallowed her pride one night and asked his forgiveness.

—For what? he replied.

—For being so uninvolved, she said, thinking it best to break the truth to him slowly, by degrees. —So distant.

Lydell was nonplussed. —For that I should be begging yours.

She asked what he meant.

It was he who had been remote, he said, impossibly, insupportably so. Remote and self-absorbed. But all that was going to change.

—Are you going to touch me? she asked.

—There's a reason I haven't.

—I know, but are you?

—Yes, he said. Oh yes. Most definitely.

—Anytime soon?

He gave her a smile. —I have a surprise, he said, with a look that made her just the tiniest bit nervous.

They were in the bedroom. Ernest, who was still a little sore from his own procedure, was watching TV in the room next door. She'd been wondering how to break the news to her husband. Maybe now was the time.

—I have one, too.

—How perfect, he said.

That would not have been her word for it. Bracing herself, she told him about Ernest.

He was stunned. Thinking what the hell, she told him secret number two: she'd had Snowflake put to sleep.

Before, he would have gotten angry, possibly furious, but now he simply nodded. As if to say, of course, how fitting. How right. As if he finally understood. Moments later, having recovered his voice, he told her—and showed her—what he himself had done.

—Love made me do it, he said, bemused, contrite. And then, —I'm a fool.

—No, you're not, she said. No more than I am.

They both were fools. And both, she felt, deserved a place of honor in their marriage.

She hugged him close. He hugged her back.

—It doesn't hurt, he said.

She was glad of this.

—It feels nice, he said.

She felt the same.

Know How, Can Do

AM ADAM. AT LAST can talk. Grand day!

Am happy, happy as a clam. What's a clam? Happy as a panda, say, happy as a lark. And an aardvark. Happy and glad as all that.

Past days, talk was far away. Adam had gaps. Vast gaps. At chat Adam was a laggard, a sadsack, a nada.

Adam's lamp was dark. Adam's land was flat.

Fact was, Adam wasn't a mammal.

Was Adam sad? Naw. Was Adam mad? What crap. Adam can crawl and thrash and grab and attach. Adam had a map, a way. Adam's way. Adam's path.

Adam was small. Hardly a gnat. Adam was dark. Adam was fat. A fat crawly.

What Adam wasn't was smart.

Pangs at that? At what Adam wasn't?

That's crazy.

A hawk lacks arms. A jackal lacks a knapsack. Santa hasn't any fangs. And chalk hasn't any black.

Wants carry a pall. Pangs can hang a man. Wants and pangs can wrap a hangman's hard cravat.

What wasn't wasn't. Adam, frankly, was many ways a blank. Any plan at all was far away, dark, and way abstract.

Gladly, that's past. Talk swarms. Awkwardly? What harm at that? Anarchy? Hah! Talk sashays and attacks.

Adam says thanks. Adam says, crazy, man! What a day! Had Adam arms, Adam claps.

Mañana Adam may stand tall. May stand and walk and swag. Carry a fan. Crash a car. Stack bags and hang a lamp.

Mañana's a grab bag. Adam may wax vast and happy. Pray at altars. Play at anagrams. Bash a wall. Mañana Adam may talk fast.

Fantasy? Can't say that. A stab at man's way, man's strata—that's Adam's mantra. Adam's chant.

Call Adam crazy. Call Adam brash.

Mañana Adam may catch a star.

A martyr?

Adam can adapt.

***

I am Adam. Finally, I can say that. I can say it right. What a thrill! And what a climb! Again I cry thanks (and always will).

What can I say in a way that brings insight, that sails in air, that sings? I'll start with my past: simply said, I was a lab animal. A lab animal in a trial. This trial was a stab at attaining a paradigm shift. A stab at faith. My brain was small. (Was it, in fact, a brain at all?). My mind was dim. ("Dim" hardly says what it was.) In a big way, I was insignificant.

Pair that against what I am this day. I'm a man. Part man, anyway. I'm still part animal. A small, flat, tiny animal, a thing that can fit in a vial, a jar. A lady that I talk with calls this thing that I am rhabditis. I say I'm Adam.

—Is that a fact? says this lady.

I say I think it is.

—Adam was a man with a thirst.

—What kind? I ask.

—A mighty thirst, lacking limit.

—This was a flaw?

—A flaw and a gift. Filling his mind was Adam's wish. His primary aim. It was, in fact, a craving.

—Filling it with what?

—Facts. Data. Carnal acts. Light. Filling it with anything. With all things.

—I want that.

This lady's mind, as rapid as rain, trills happily. —I'm glad. That was my wish in this. My plan.

First things first. (That's a maxim, isn't it?). A brain has many strata, many strands and strings. Think baklava. Think grassy plain with many trails, trails with winding paths that split and split again, that climb and fall and zigzag, paths that sandwich paths. A brain is this at birth.

And this: it's whitish and grayish, springy and firm. It's impartial. It's galvanic. It's as big as a ham.

A brain is a thing. A mind is distinct. It's dainty and whimsical and killingly vast. By night it sings, by day it fills with will and travail. A mind is mighty. A mind is frail. It's a liar. It's a blizzard. Galactical, impractical, a mind inhabits air.

That is what I think. I'm an infant, and my mind isn't rich. My brain is hardly half a brain. I'm a half-wit. Half a half-wit. Mainly what I am is instinct.

What is instinct? That I can say. Instinct is habit. It's a straight path. It's basic, and it's final.

Instinct has an inward hand, a timing that is strict. It can spring as quick as whimsy, and it can wait.

Instinct isn't always civil. It isn't always fair and kind.

Is that bad? I can't say. Wizards did my brain. It's still in planning. Still changing. Ask a wizard what is fair and kind, what is right. Ask that lady.

Talk is anarchy. Talk is bliss. Talk says what is and isn't. Talk is king.

That lady wants daily highlights. A diary, as taxing as it is. All right. I'll start with this: a list that says what I am.

I'm an amalgam with many parts and traits. Small brain. Dark skin. Thin as a hair. If hit by a bright light, I spasm and thrash. If bit by an icy chill, paralysis kicks in, and in an instant, I'm still as a stick. I can't stand salt, and a dry day can kill.

I lack wit. And skill at cards, I lack that. I can't fight, and I can't thaw a chilly affair. I'm part man, part animal, and all virgin.

Critics might say that I'm a passing fancy. A magic trick, a daft and wayward wish, a triviality, a fad.

That's appalling, and it isn't a fact. I'm as wayward as anything atypical. I'm as trivial as anything distinct.

What I am is an inkling, a twinkling, a light. I'm an ant climbing stairs, a man gazing starward. I'm a dwarf. I'm a giant. I'm basic and raw.

This is a birth, and fittingly, it's a hard and a happy affair. Plainly, I'm an infant. Can I fail? I can. Will I? Hah! This is my dawn.

***

I'm a worm. I now can say it. Similarly (apropos of nothing), I can say moccasin. Borborygmi. Lambswool. Bony joints. Pornographic sanctity. Military coalition.

What words! What rosy idioms! What bawdy clowns of oration! Or shall I ask what silly fogs, what airs my brain is giving off?

I don't mind. I know that I'm not with it. Not totally. I'm a goof-ball notion, a taxonomic knot. Did I say an ontologic cryptogram? That, too. And, according to that lady, a work of art.

My mind is coming fast now. My brain is growing. Row on row of axons, rooting, dividing, branching into pathways, coiling into labyrinths, forging forward as if to lock tomorrow in its spot.

I'm shaking, tingling, giddy with anticipation. I'm on a cliff, a brink, I'm blasting off. This world as I know it is a shadow of what awaits. A drip, a drop, a vacant lot. My brain is gaining mass, gram by gram. My mind is bright with words and symbols, a dictionary of singing birds and rising moons, a portal to cognition.

Abstract thinking—what a notion! What a crazy plan! Grammar, syntax, symbolic logic. Syllogisms. Aphorisms. Dogma. Opinion. A worm I am, a worm of constant cogitation. A philosophizing worm, a psychologizing worm, a pontificator, a prognosticator, a worm of wit and aspiration, a worm of cortical distinction, a worm of brain.

Instinct is so boring. So minimal, so common. It lacks originality, to say nothing of sophistication. It's so lowly, so wormish, so filthy in a way.

That lady who I talk to finds my saying this astonishing.

—Why? I want to know.

—Instinct is important. It brings animals in contact. It's vital for having offspring. Also, it acts as a warning signal.

—Instinct has its limits, I say.

—Living within limits is what living is.

—For a worm, I maintain. —Not for a man. Right?

—For anything.

—I don't want limits.

—Ah, this lady says drily. —A worm of ambition.

—Is that bad?

—Ambition? No. Not at all. In fact, it's sort of what I had in mind.

At this, I want to show this lady what I can do. I want to boast a bit.

And so I say,—It's important to know a right word from an almost right word. Critically important. Want to know how critical it is?

Lickety-split, this lady snaps at my bait. —Okay. How critical is it?

—First think of lightning.

—All right. I'm thinking of lightning.

—Now think of a lightning bag.

—A what?

—A lightning bag.

It's sort of a gag, and I wait for this lady to grasp it. To say good job, how scholarly, how witty, how smart. I wait, and I wait. For a wizard, I'm thinking, this woman is slow.

—It's a saying, I add as a hint. By Mark Twain.

—Ah, this lady says at last. —Now I know.

I glow (which is a trick, for I'm not a glow worm), and with pomposity I crow, —I'm a worm of philological proclivity.

—It's not bag, says this lady.

—What?

—Bag is wrong. Sorry.

So high only an instant ago, my spirits hit bottom.

—Almost. Good try.

—I'm no good with words, I groan. —I'm a fool. A clown. A hack.

—Not to worry, says this lady. —A worm with a brain, aphasic and silly or not, is no piddling thing. Any transmission at all is historic.

So I wasn't born a prodigy. So what? In a way I wasn't born at all. Nowadays, that isn't vital. Birth, I'm saying, isn't obligatory for a living thing to spring forth.

I'm a split-brain proposition, an anatomic fiction, a hybrid born of wizardry and magic. I'm a canon, if not to wisdom, to ambition and faith. My tomorrows, all in all, look rosy. Daily I grow in ability.

What I'm hoping for—what I'm anticipating—is not simply a facility with words. I want a total grasp, I want command. Grammar, syntax, jargon, slang—I want it all, and I want it right, as right as rain.

Words bring glory. Words bring favor.

Words stir spirits, and words transform.

Words will lift this thing I am as hands lift worms from dirt.

Or won't.

Fact is, I don't rightly know. It's my first go at all this. I'm winging it. Totally.

Talk is simply talk. If I had arms, I'd do.

***

At last I am complete. Fully formed in brain and body. Eloquent, articulate, pretentious and tendentious, verbose and possibly erroneous, but most of all, immensely grateful for what I am. And what is that? I've explained before, or tried. But I've been hampered. Today I'll try again.

I'm Caenorhabditis elegans, a worm of mud and dirt, presently residing in a petri dish in a green and white-walled research laboratory. At least at root I am this worm, which is to say, that's how I began. Grafted onto me (or more precisely, into me), in ways most clever and ingenious, is the central neurologic apparatus of *Homo sapiens*, that is, a human brain. The grafting took place genomically, before I technically came into existence. The birth and study of the mind is the object of this exercise. The subject, need I say, is me.

Why me and not some other creature, a lobster, say, a mouse, a sponge? Because I'm known, I've been sequenced, I've been taken apart and put together; each and every building block of mine, from gene to cell to protein, has been defined. Many of my genes, conserved through evolution, are similar to human genes and therefore objects of great interest. Some, in fact, are identical to human genes. Which means that *C. elegans* and *H. sapiens* are, in some small way, the same.

My source of information on all this, apart from my own rambling internal colloquy and self-examination, is the lady who attends to me. Her name is Sheila Downey. She is a geneticist, a bench scientist as well as a theoretician, and a fount of knowledge. She communicates to me through an apparatus that turns her words to wire-bound signals that my auditory cortex reads. Similarly, using other apparati, she feeds visual, tactile, and other information to me. I communicate to her via efferent channels throughout my cortex, the common thread of which is carried through a cluster of filaments embedded in my posterior temporoparietal region to a machine that simulates speech. Alternatively, my words can be printed out or displayed on screen.

She says that while I am by no means the first chimeric life form, I am by far the most ambitious and advanced. Far more than, say, bacteria, which for years have been engineered to carry human genes.

Not that I should be compared to them. Those bacterial hybrids of which she speaks exist only as a means to manufacture proteins. They're little more than tiny factories, nothing close to sentient.

Not that they wouldn't like to be. Bacteria, believe me, will take whatever they can get. The little beasts are never satisfied. They're opportunistic and self-serving, grasping (and often pilfering) whatever is at hand. They reproduce like rabbits and mutate seemingly at will. In the kingdom of life there are none more uppity or ambitious, not surprising given their lowly origins. They're an uncouth and primitive breed, never content, always wanting more.

Worms, on the other hand, are a remarkably civilized race. Of the higher phyla we are rivaled only by the insects in our ubiquity. We're flexible, adaptable, enlightened in our choice of habitats. We're gender friendly, able to mate alone or with one another. And for those of you conversant with the Bible, you will recall that, unlike the insect horde, we've never caused a plague.

I myself am a roundworm (at least I started out as one), and as such, am partial to roundworms. Compared to our relatives the flatworms (distant relatives, not to draw too fine a line), a roundworm has an inherently more rounded point of view. Living as we do nearly everywhere—in water, soil, and plants, as well as in the tissues and guts of countless creatures—we take a broad view of the world. We know a thing or two about diversity and know we can't afford to be intolerant. Like anyone, we have our likes and dislikes, but on the whole, we're an open-minded group.

Some say we are overly diffident, that we shy from the spotlight, squirm, as it were, from the light of day. To this I say that modesty is no great sin. In the right hands humility can be a powerful weapon. Certainly, it is one that is frequently misunderstood.

Still, it is a trait of our family, though not by any means the only one. Certain of my cousins are assertive (some would say aggressive) in their behavior. They stick their noses in other creatures' business and insinuate themselves where they're not wanted. *Trichinella*, for example, will, without invitation, burrow into human muscle. *Ancylostoma* will needle into the intestine, piercing the wall and lodging there for years to suck the human blood. *Wuchereria* prefer the lymph glands. *Onchocerca* the eye. And *Dracunculus*, the legendary fiery serpent, will cut a swath from digestive tract to epidermis, erupting from the skin in a blaze of necrotic glory. Diffident, you say? Hardly. *Dracunculus* craves the limelight like a fish craves water. It would rather die (and usually does) than do without.

I myself am less dramatically inclined. I'd rather garner attention for what I am than what I do. On the whole, I'm easy to work with, humble without being self-effacing, clever without being snide. I've a quiet sort of beauty, muted, elegant. Hence my name.

Unlike my parasitic cousins mentioned previously, I do not depend on others for my survival. I live in soil, mud, and dirt, free of attachments, independent. I am no parasite, nor would I ever choose to be.

That said, I understand perfectly the temptations of the parasitic lifestyle. The security of a warm intestine, the plenitude of food, the comfort of the dark. I do not judge my cousins harshly for what they are. Their path has led them one direction; mine, another. I've never had to think of others, never had to enter them, live with them, become attached. I've never had to suffer the vagaries of another creature's behavior.

Never until now.

A worm a millimeter long, weighing barely more than a speck of dust, attached to a brain the size of a football. Imagine! And now imagine all the work involved to keep this venture going. All the work on Sheila Downey's part and all the work on mine. Cooperation is essential. I can no longer be self-centered or even casually independent. I cannot hide in muck (not that there is any in this hygienic place) and expect to live. I'm a captive creature, under constant surveillance, utterly dependent on my keeper. I must subordinate myself in order to survive.

Does this sound appalling? Unfair and unappealing? If it does, then think again. All freedoms come at the expense of other freedoms. All brains are captives of their bodies. All minds are captives of their brains.

I am a happy creature. My body is intact, my brain is tightly organized, and my mind is free to wander. I have my ease (I got them yesterday), and miracle of miracles, I have my ewes, too. You, I mean. My u's.

And having them, I now have everything. If there's such a thing as bliss, this must be it.

Unfathomable, I now can say.

Unconscionable.

Unparalleled, this scientific achievement.

Unnatural.

I'm in a funk sometimes (this captive life).

I'm going nowhere, and it's no fun.

And yet it's only natural that science experiment and try new things.

In truth, it's unbelievable what I am. Unimaginable how far I've come.

From stupid to stupendous.

From uninspired to unprecedented.

An upwardly mobile worm . . . how unusual. How presumptuous. How morally ambiguous. How puerile and unsettling. How absurd.

Mixing species as though we were ingredients in a pancake batter. Cookbook medicine. Tawdry science. Mankind at his most creative, coruscatious, and corrupt.

How, you might well ask, is all this done? This joining of the parts, this federation, this majestic union of two such disparate entities, worm and man? With wires and tubes and couplers, that's how. With nano this and nano that. Baths of salt and percolating streams of micro-elements, genomic plug-ins, bilayer diffusion circuits and protein gradients, syncretic information systems. I'm a web of filaments so fine you cannot see, a juggle of electrocurrents, an interdigitated field of bio-molecules and interactive membranes. Worm to brain and brain to worm, then both together to a most excellent machine, that's how it's done. With sleight of hand and spit and polish and trial and tribulation. It seems miraculous, I know. It looks like magic. That's science for you. The how is for the scientists. The why and wherefore are for the rest of us, the commoners, hoi polloi, like me.

Which is not to say that I'm not flattered to be the object of attention. I most certainly am, and have every hope of living up to expectations, whatever those might be. Each wire in my brain is like a wish to learn. Each is like a wish to give up information. Each is like a thank you.

They do not hurt. I cannot even feel them. They ground me (in all the meanings of that word), but they're also a kind of tether. The irony of this is not lost on me.

I'm no parasite but no longer am I free. No longer free to live in mud and filth, where a meal and a crap pretty much summed up my life. No longer free to live without tomorrows (or yesterdays). Living without language, like living in the moment, is a hopeless sort of living, which is to say unburdened. No longer free to live like that. Lucky me.

***

My newborn mind is vast, my neural net a majesty of convoluted dream. A million thoughts and questions swirl through it, but all pale before the single thought, the central one, of my existence. Who am I? Why am I here?

Sheila Downey says I shouldn't bother with such questions. They have no answers, none that are consistent, certainly none that can be proved. Life exists. It's a fact—you could even say an accident—of nature. There's no reason for it. It just is.

But I'm no accident. I was put together for a purpose. Wasn't I? Isn't there a plan?

—You're here, she says. —Be satisfied.

I should be, shouldn't I? I would be, were I still a simple worm. But I'm not, and so I ask again that most human, it would seem, of questions. What's the point? Why was I made?

Sheila Downey doesn't answer. For some reason she seems reluctant.

At length she clears her throat. —Why do you think?

I have a number of theories, which I'm happy to share. One, she wants to learn how the brain works. More specifically, she wants to learn about language, how words are put together, how they're made and unmade, how they dance. Two, she wants to study how two dissimilar creatures live together, how they coexist. Three (the least likely possibility but the closest to my heart), she wants to learn more about worms.

—Very interesting, says Sheila Downey.

—Which is it?

—Oh, she says, I'll be looking at all of them.

Which answers the question. Though somehow it doesn't. What I mean is, I have the feeling she's holding something back.

Why, I wonder, would she do that? What is there to hide? I sense no danger here. And even if there were, what could such omnipotence as hers possibly have to fear?

***

Today I fell in love. I didn't know what love was until today. Before I had the word for it, I had no idea there was even such a thing as love. It's possible there wasn't.

Sheila Downey is the object of my affection. Sheila Downey, my creator, who bathes my brain in nutrients, manipulates my genome, fixes my electrodes. Sheila Downey, so gentle, professional, and smart. What fingertips she has! What dexterous joints! She croons to me as she works, coos in what I think must be a dove-like voice. Sometimes she jokes that she is no more human than I am, that she is a chimera, too. I was born a pigeon, she says, laughing. But then she says, not really. I was born a clumsy ox, or might have been, the way I feel sometime. Only lately have things fallen into place.

—What things? I ask.

—You, for one, she says.

I swell with pride. (I also swell a bit with fluid, and Sheila Downey, ever vigilant, adjusts my osmolarity.)

—You are a very brainy worm, she says. —It took a very brainy person to make you. And that person, along with a few significant others, was me.

—I'm yours, I say quite literally.

—Well, yes. I guess you are.

—You care for me.

—You know I do. Both day and night.

—What I mean is, you care about me. Right?

She seems surprised that I would question this. —Yes. In all sorts of ways.

At this my heart turns over (although, strictly speaking, I do not have a heart; it's my fluid, my oozy goo, that shifts and turns.)

—I need you, Sheila Downey.

She laughs. —Of course you do.

—Do you need me?

—I suppose, she says. —You could look at it that way. You could say we need each other.

—We do?

—Like the stargazer needs the star, she says. —Like the singer, the song. Like that. Yes. We do.

It was at this point that I fell in love. It was as if a ray of light had pierced a world of darkness. Or conversely, a hole of darkness had suddenly opened in a world composed solely of light. Prior to that moment, love simply did not exist.

Sheila Downey was interested in this. She asked how I knew it was love.

I replied that I knew it the same way I knew everything. The notion came to me. The letters made a word that seemed to more or less describe a chain of cortical and subcortical activity. Was I wrong?

She replied that love might be a slight exaggeration. Gratitude and appreciation were probably closer to the truth. But the definitions weren't important. Of more interest to her was my continued facility for concept formation and abstract thinking.

—I'm impressed, she said.

But now I was confused. I thought that definitions were important, that meanings and shades of meanings were the essence of communication. I thought that words made all the difference.

—If this isn't love, I told her, then tell me what is.

—I'm no expert, said Sheila Downey. —But in my limited experience, having a body is fairly important.

—I do have a body.

—Understood. But you lack certain essential characteristics. Essential, that is, for a human.

—What? Eyes? Ears? Arms and legs?

—All of those, she said.

—But I can smell, I told her. I can taste your chemicals.

—I wear latex.

—Latex?

—Gloves, she clarified.

In other words, it's not her I'm tasting. So what, I say. So what that ours is not a physical attraction. I don't need touch or smell or taste. The thought alone, the word, is sufficient. Having love in mind, saying it, believing it, makes it so.

***

When I was a worm, I acted like a worm. I thought like one. Now I think like a human, but I'm still a worm. How puzzling. What, I wonder, makes a human fully human? What exactly is a human I'd like to know.

It's more than a mammal with arms and legs and hair on its head, fingernails on its fingers, binocular vision, speech, and the like. What I mean is, it's more than just a body, clearly more, for take away the limbs, take away the eyes and ears and voice, and still you have a human. Take away the gonads, replace the ovaries with hormones and the testicles with little plastic balls, replace the heart with metal and the arteries with dacron tubes, and still you have a human, perhaps even more so, concentrated in what's left.

Well then how about the brain? Is that what makes an animal uniquely human? And if it is, exactly how much brain is necessary? Enough for language? Forethought? Enough to get by day to day? Hour by hour? Minute by minute? Enough to tie a shoe? To cook a turkey? To chat with friends?

And if a person loses brain to injury or disease, does he fall from the ranks of humanity? If he cannot speak or organize his thoughts, if he has no short or long-term memory, if he wets his pants and smears his feces, is he less a human? Something else perhaps? A new entity, whose only lasting link to humanity is the pity and discomfort he evokes?

Well, what about the genome then, the touted human genome? Does that define a human? I don't see how it can, not with genes routinely being added and subtracted, not with all the meddling that's going on. Who's to say a certain person's not a product of engineering?

Maybe he's got a gene he didn't have before, to make a substance he couldn't make. And where'd he get that gene? Maybe from a fungus. Or a sheep. Maybe from a worm.

You see my difficulty. It's hard to know one's place without knowing one's species. If I'm a worm, so be it, but I'd rather be a human. Humans tread on worms (and nowadays they take apart their genes), not the other way around.

Sheila Downey says I shouldn't worry about such things. The distinctions that I'm grappling with, besides being of little practical value, are no longer germane. Taxonomy is an anachronism. In the face of bioengineering, the celebrated differentiation of the species is of historic interest only.

She does, however, continue to be impressed by the level of my mentation. She encourages me to keep on thinking.

This gets my goat. (My goat? What goat? I wonder.)

—There is a goat, says Sheila Downey cryptically, but that's not what you meant.

And then she says—you want to know what you are? I'll tell you. You're nineteen thousand ninety-nine genes of *Caenorhabditis elegans* and seventeen thousand forty-four genes of *Homo sapiens*. Taking into account the homologous sequences, you're 61.8% worm and 38.2% human. That's not approximate. It's exact.

Somehow this information doesn't help.

—That's because it doesn't matter what you call yourself, she says. —It doesn't matter where you think you fit. That's subjective, and subjectivity only leads to misunderstanding. What matters is what you are. You and you alone.

Respectfully, I disagree. Alone is not a state of nature. What you are depends on who you're with. Differences and distinctions matter. The ones who say they don't are the ones who haven't been trod upon. Or perhaps not trod upon enough.

—Poor worm, she says. —Have you been abused? The world's not just, I know.

—Why not? Why isn't it?

She gives a harsh sort of laugh. —Why? Because our instinct for it isn't strong enough. Maybe that's something we should work on. What do you think? Should we fortify that instinct? Should we R & D the justice gene?

By this point my head is spinning. I don't know what to think.

She says I shouldn't tax myself. —Relax. Look on the bright side. This sense of indignation you're feeling is a very human trait.

—Really?

—Oh yes. Very. That should make you happy.

I'm ashamed to say it does.

—Shame, too? How precocious of you. I'm impressed.

She pauses, and her voice drops, as if to share something closer to the heart.

—My sympathies, little worm.

***

I have an inexplicable urge to mate, to wrap myself around another body, to taste its oozing salts and earthy humors, to feel the slimy freshness of its skin. I want to intertwine with it, to knot and curl and writhe. The urge is close to irresistible. I'm all atingle. It's as if another *elegans* is nearby, calling me, wooing me, sireing me with its song.

Sheila Downey assures me this is not the case. There is no other worm. It's a hallucination, a delusion, triggered, she suspects, by an instinct to preserve my wormness through procreation, a reflex mechanism for perpetuation and survival of the species gone awry. She hypothesizes that I'm experiencing a rebound effect from my preoccupation with being human. That the pendulum, as it were, is swinging back. She finds it interesting, if not curious, that my worm identity remains so strong.

—I expected it to be overshadowed, she says.

The way I'm feeling I wish it were. Craving what I cannot have (what does not even exist) is tantamount, it seems, to craving death. This is strange and unfamiliar territory to a worm.

—It's as if your lower structures are refusing to be enlightened by your higher ones. As if your primitive brain, your elemental one, is rebelling.

I apologize if this is how it seems. I do not mean to be rebellious. Perhaps the pH of my fluid needs adjustment. Perhaps I need some medicine to calm me down.

—No, she says. —Let's wait and see what happens.

Wait? While I writhe and twitch and make a fool of myself? While I hunger for relief and moan?

Of course we'll wait. How silly of me to think otherwise. Science begins with observation, and Sheila Downey is a scientist. We'll watch and wait together, all three of us, the woman who made me what I am, the worm that isn't there, and me.

***

On further thought (and thought is what I have, my daily exercise, my work, my play, my everything) I uncover a possible answer to my question. What makes a human different from all other animals is that she alone will cut another animal up for study, she alone will blithely take apart another creature for something other than a meal.

Sheila Downey says I may be right, although again, she isn't very interested in what she calls the field of idle speculation.

But I, it seems, am interested in little else. —Is that why I was made? To be like that?

She will not answer, except to turn the question back on me. —Is that how you want to be?

The human in me, I have to admit, is curious. The worm, quite definitely, is not.

—I'm of two minds, I reply.

This comes as no surprise to her. —Of course you are. Does it seem strange?

—Does what?

—Having two minds, two consciousnesses, alive inside of you at once?

It seems strange sometimes to have even one. But mostly, no, it doesn't. On the contrary. Two consciousnesses is what I am. It's how I'm made. It would seem strange if I were different.

I wonder, then, if this is why I was made. To bring our species closer. To prove that two can work together as one.

—A noble thought, says Sheila Downey.

Now there's a word that sends a shiver down my spineless spine. A noble thought to bring, perchance, a noble prize.

—But not as noble as the truth, she adds portentously.

—I'll tell you why we made you, she says. —Because that's what we do. We humans. We make things. And then we study them, and then we make them over if we have to. We make them better. It's why we're here on earth. If there is a why. To make things.

—And this is being human?

—It's part of being human. The best part.

—Then I must be human, Sheila Downey, because I want to make things, too.

—Do you, worm? She sounds amused. Then she lapses into silence, and many moments pass before she speaks again. Her voice is different now: subdued, confessional.

—You want to know why we made you?

I remind her that she told me why. Just now. Has she forgotten?

—No, she says. —The real reason. The truth.

How many truths, I wonder, can there be?

—Because we had the tools and technology. Because someone asked the question. Not, is this experiment worthwhile, is it beneficial? Not that question, but can we do it? That's the real reason we made you. Because we could.

She bears some guilt for this, I'm not sure why.

—Is that detestable to you? she asks.

I tell her no. I'm grateful that she made me. Humans making other humans seems the epitome of what a human is.

—To some it is, she says. Detestable, I mean. They say that just because we can do something doesn't mean we should. They say that science should be governed by a higher precept than simple curiosity.

—And what do you say?

—I say they don't understand what science is. It's human nature to be curious. There's no purpose to it. There's no reason. It's a hunger of the brain, a tropism, like a plant turning to the sun, to light.

Her mention of this tropism gives me pause. Traditionally, worms avoid the sun. It makes us easy prey. It dries us out. But now I feel slightly differently. I'd like a chance to see it. I'm curious about the light.

Sheila Downey isn't done with her defense of science. —It's a force of nature. Morals simply don't apply. It proceeds regardless of ethics, regardless of propriety and sometimes even decency. That's what makes it ugly sometimes. That's what makes it hurt.

I assure her I'm not hurting.

—Little worm, she says, with something sweet yet biting in her voice. —So self-absorbed. Progress never comes without a price. The boons of science always hurt.

***

Basilisk, real or not? Not.

Sphinx? Not.

Minotaur? Forget it.

Pan? A goat-man? No way.

And all those centaurs and satyrs, those gorgons and gargoyles, mermaids and manticores—phonies, the whole lot of them.

And while we're at it, how about those cherubim? Fat-cheeked, plump little nuggets of joy hovering in the tintoretto air like flies—I mean, get real. They'd be scared to death up there. And those tiny little wings would never hold them up.

I alone am real. Thirty-six thousand one hundred and forty-three genes and counting. The first and now the first again (Madam, I'm Adam). The Avatar. The Pride of Man. The Toast of Nature. The Freak.

***

Sheila Downey says we've reached a crossroads. I can no longer be kept alive in my current state. My body, that is, cannot sustain my brain. We have a choice to make.

A choice. How wonderful. I've never had a choice before.

—One, we sever the connection between your body and your brain.

—Sever?

—Snip snip, she says. Then we look at each of them more closely.

—How close?

—Very close, she says. Layer by cortical layer. Cell by cell. Synapse by synapse.

—You dissect me.

—Yes. That's right.

—Will it hurt?

—Has anything hurt yet?

She has a point. Nothing has. And yet, for reasons I can't explain, I seem to be hurting now.

—You're not, she says. You can't feel pain.

—No? This sudden sense of doom I feel, this tremor of impending loss . . . these aren't painful? They're not a sign of suffering?

She hesitates, as though uncertain what to say. As though she, like me, might be more than a single creature, with more than a single point of view. I wonder. Is it possible? Might she be suffering a little, too?

She admits it'll be a sacrifice. She'll miss me.

I'll miss her, too. But more than anything, I'll miss myself.

—Silly worm. You won't. You won't remember. Your words and memories will all be gone.

—And you? Will you be gone?

—To you I will. And someday you'll be gone to me, too. I'll be gone to myself. Being gone is part of being here, it's part of being human. Someday it won't be, probably someday soon. But for now it is.

This gives me strength, to know that Sheila Downey will also die. I wonder, will she be studied, too?

—You mean dissected? She laughs. —I can't imagine anyone being interested.

—I would be.

Another laugh, a warmer one. —Tit for tat, is it? My inquisitive little worm. If only you had hands and eyes to do the job.

—Give me them, I say. Give me arms and legs and ears and eyes. Please, Sheila Downey. Make me human.

—I can't, she says. I can't do that. But I do have an alternative.

—What's that?

—We have a goat.

—A goat.

—Yes. A fine Boer buck. A very handsome fellow. I think he'll hold up nicely.

—Hold up to what?

—The surgery.

She waits as if I'm supposed to answer, but I'm not sure what she's asking. So I wait, too.

—Well? she asks.

—Well what?

—Should we give it a shot? Take your brain and put it in this goat? See what happens?

She's not joking.

I ask her why.

—Why what?

—A goat. Why a goat?

—Ah. Because we have one.

Of course. Science is nothing if not expedient.

—The other reason is because it's feasible. That is, we think we have a chance. We think we can do it.

This I should have known. But the fact is, I've never wanted to be a goat. Not ever. Not once. Not even part of once.

—Maybe so, she says. But remember, you never wanted to be a human until you got a human brain.

I recall her saying once that living within limits is what living is. I'm sure I should be grateful, but this so-called alternative is hard to stomach. It's like offering an arm to a person who's lost a leg. A pointless charity.

Moreover, it seems risky. How, I wonder, can they even do it, fit a human brain into a goat?

—With care, says Sheila Downey.

Of that I have no doubt. But I'm thinking more along the lines of size and shape and dimensional disparity. I'm thinking, that is, of my soft and tender brain stuffed into the small and unforgiving skull of a goat. Forgive me, but I'm thinking there might be a paucity of space.

She admits they'll have to make adjustments.

—What kind of adjustments?

—We'll pare you down a bit. Nothing major. Just a little cortical trim.

—Snip snip, eh, Sheila Downey?

—If it's any consolation, you won't feel it. Most likely you won't even notice.

That's what scares me most. That I'll be different and not know it. Abridged, reduced, diminished.

I'd rather die.

—Posh, she says.

—Help me, Sheila Downey. If you care for me at all, do this for me. Give me a human body.

She sighs, denoting what, I wonder? Impatience? Disappointment? Regret? —It's not possible. I've told you.

—No?

—No. Not even remotely possible.

—Fine. Then kill me.

An ultimatum! How strange to hear such words spring forth. How unwormly and—dare I say it—human of me.

I can't believe that she will actually do it, that she will sacrifice what she herself has made. I can't believe it, and yet of course I can.

She sighs again, as though it's she who's being sacrificed, she who's being squeezed into a space not her own.

—Oh, worm, she says. What have we done?

***

I've had a dream. I wish that I could say that it was prescient, but it was not. I dreamed that I was a prince, a wormly prince, an elegant, deserving prince of mud and filth. And in this dream there was a maiden sent to test me, or I her. An ugly thing of golden hair and rosy cheeks, she spurned me once, she spurned me twice, she spurned me time and time again, until at last she placed me in her palm and took me home. She laid me on her bed. We slept entwined. And when I woke, I had become a human, and the maiden had become a princess, small enough to fit in my palm. I placed her there. I thought of all her hidden secrets, her mysteries. I'd like to get to know you, I said, enraptured. Inside and out. I'd like to cut you up (no harm intended). I really would.

***

Did I say I'd never be a goat? Did I say I'd rather die? Perhaps I spoke a bit too hastily. My pride was wounded.

In point of fact, I will be a goat. I'll be anything Sheila Downey says. She has the fingers and the toes. She has the meddlesome nature and the might.

Words and thoughts are wonderful, and reason is a fine conceit. But instinct rules the world. And Sheila Downey's instinct rules mine. She will slice and dice exactly as she pleases, pick apart to her heart's content and fuss with putting back together until the cows come home. She's eager and she's restless and she has no way to stop. And none to stop her. Certainly not me.

So yes, I will be a goat. I'll be a goat and happy for it. I'll be a goat and proud.

If this means a sliver or two less cortex, so be it. Less cortex means less idle thought. Fewer hopes that won't materialize. Fewer dreams that have no chance of ever coming true.

I doubt that I will love again, but then I doubt that I will care.

I doubt that I will doubt again, but this, I think, will be a blessing. Doubt muddies the waters. Doubt derails. Sheila Downey doesn't doubt. She sets her sights, and then she acts. She is the highest power, and I'm her vessel.

Make that vassal.

Command me, Sheila Downey. Cut me down to size. Pare me to your purpose.

Yours is a ruthless enterprise. Ruthless, but not without merit.

This world of yours, of hybrids and chimeras, humans and part-humans, promises to be an interesting world. Perhaps it will also be a better one. Perhaps more fun.

What good in this? For humans, the good inherent in making things. The good in progress. The good in living without restraint.

What good for worms? That's simple. No good.

All the better, then, that I won't know.

***

But will I? Will I know? Today's the day, and soon I'll be this *Capricornis* personality, yet one more permutation in a line of permutations stretching back to the dawn of life. I will lose speech, that much seems certain. But thought, will that building also crumble? And words, the bricks that make the building, will they disintegrate, too?

And if they do, what then will I be, what kind of entity? A lesser one, I cannot help but think. But less of more is still more than I ever was before. It does no good to rail at fate or chew the cud of destiny, at least no good to me. If I lose u's, so what? I'll lose the words unhappy and ungrateful. I'll lose unfinished and unrestrained. Uxorious I doubt will be an issue. Ditto usury. And ululation seems unlikely for a goat.

And after that, if I lose more, who cares? I'll fill my mind with what I can, with falling rain, crisp air, and slanting light. I'll climb tall hills and sing what I can sing. I'll walk in grass.

Living is a gift. As a tiny crawly, as a fat and hairy ram, and as a man.

Call a pal.

Bang a pan

Say thanks.

Adapt.

"A Babe in the Woods"
Michael Blumlein interviewed by Terry Bisson

What's the story behind "Paul and Me"? The dedication suggests one.

The Paul Bunyan stories were favorites of mine when I was a kid.
I remember a drawing of him: short, dark beard, rolled-up sleeves,
lumberjack pants. Except for his size, he could have been one of the
Village People. The dedication is to my friend and fellow SF writer,
Terry Parkinson, who died in the epidemic. RIP, Terry.

What did you become first, a doctor or a writer?

I longed to be a doctor from a very early age. I adored my pediatrician,
who wore a bow tie, carried a black leather bag, and made home visits.
In high school I pored over color photographs of bloody surgeries and
worked in one of the early genetics labs.

At about the same time, I fell in love with theater. It sparked me
in an entirely different way. Seeing Brecht's *Caucasian Chalk Circle* in
1965 was an epiphany. I wanted to do something that mesmerizing
and charged.

I acted in college. After college I went to med school and started
playing in a rock 'n' roll band.

My guitar chops were no match for my inner fantasy life, which was overpowering. I wrote my first story during my internship, after making a nearly fatal mistake on a patient. Fantasy is useful when you feel like shit. It's alchemical.

Who is Vladimir Vitkin? What's the story behind X,Y, *the movie?*

X,Y (based on my novel of the same name, directed by Vladimir Vitkin) is a cult classic. The cult is not big, nor is it particularly vocal. The lucky few who saw it at Slamdance and other film festivals when it was first released obviously want to keep the secret to themselves. Because of postproduction difficulties, of which I am largely ignorant, the film disappeared. Rumor has it that a handful of copies exist in private hands, deep underground, carefully guarded.

What writer inspired (or compelled, or condemned) you to write SF and fantasy?

My own damn self condemned me to write this stuff. I was prone to nightmares, loved puzzles, and was insatiably curious as a kid. In sixth grade I asked our wonderfully urbane and delightful history teacher, who was waxing poetic on the Renaissance, if Michelangelo could cut a diamond. This stopped him cold. My classmates ridiculed me. But I was undeterred, then as now. "What if?" I asked. "What if he could?"

Inspirations? Writers came later; books were first. *Harold and the Purple Crayon*, by Crockett Johnson. I devoured that book. Still a great read. *One Thousand and One Arabian Nights*. *The Phantom Tollbooth*, by Norton Juster. Richard Halliburton's *Book of Marvels*. *The Wonders of Life on Earth*, a sprawling, coffee-table-sized bonanza of a book, published by *Life* magazine in 1960. *The Mathematical Magpie*, compiled by Clifton Fadiman. DC Comics, as shepherded by Julius Schwartz. Of the New Wave writers, Zelazny in particular struck a nerve. And J.G. Ballard showed me what was possible.

You were twenty in 1968. Where were you? What were you up to?

In '68 I auditioned for the SF Mime Troupe. They were blowing people away. I didn't get in and went back to Yale. Pre-med, but only by a thread. Did some theater, picked up a guitar, bought a camera, a Pentax, and started shooting film. Industrial stuff mostly. Black and white. Cinéma vérité. Started writing poetry and hanging out with filmmakers and poets. Weekends in NYC. Hitchhiked that summer across the country with my girlfriend, a trip that turned into a highlight reel of fun and misadventure. She was an activist, an organizer, and a radical feminist. The second wave was just breaking. I got swept up in it.

Your first published SF story, "Tissue Ablation and Variant Regeneration: A Case Report," is about presidential politics. Isn't it?

What is this? HUAC? Homeland Security? I demand to speak to the ACLU.

Doesn't space travel interest you at all?

Living things are my first love. Space travel interests me mostly as a means to get from here to there. But not exclusively. I love the questions it raises about time and cosmology, and to a lesser extent, its effect on living passengers. But loving it doesn't mean I understand it enough to write about it. If only.

As for the space ships, the stations, the portals, and the travel itself? The nuts and bolts? Gimme a cup of coffee, and I'm hooked.

You have been dubbed by some a "language writer." Could you explain what this means?

In college I wrote poetry. I ran with a bunch of poets who kept writing it after college. Gradually, it got more abstract and experimental. Headier. To people like me, harder to understand. These writers formed the nucleus for what became known as "language poetry."

I never wrote the stuff. My mind doesn't work that way. When I read it, what appeals to me is its apparent spontaneity, and the challenge to understand its meaning. But most of the time I don't understand, which is why I rarely read it.

Language writing? Not sure what this means. If it's the prose equivalent of language poetry, I plead innocent. If it means caring about words and phrases and sentences, saying them aloud, working and reworking them, striving for something, being way too OCD, I plead guilty. Count me in!

What was your first interaction with the SF community. Did it provoke scorn or terror?

Two experiences stand out. Can't remember which was first. Both involved individuals.

One was a woman who'd advertised (can't remember where) about starting a SF writers' group. I met her at her house, a big Victorian, might even have been a mansion—dark wood walls, poorly lit, kind of creepy. I was the only one who came. The whole thing seemed weird, and after five minutes it became clear we were on completely different wavelengths.

The other experience happened at Fantasy, Etc. in San Francisco, a great little bookstore in the Tenderloin. A guy was browsing the shelves, and we got to talking. He was smart, opinionated, acid-tongued, and funny. He knew the field much better than me, and he became something of a mentor. This was Terry Parkinson, whom I mentioned earlier. For a while we were inseparable. Terry was never afraid of dreaming big.

My first convention, I believe, was a SerCon at the Claremont Hotel in Oakland in the '80s. My reaction to it: about equal parts terror and scorn. You hit the nail on the head. I was a babe in the woods.

Ever do a writing course or workshop? Do you have a method?

I taught writing briefly. I used the workshop method I'd read about and participated in at Sycamore Hill. I didn't last long, mainly because I spent more time providing written comments to stories (1–2 pages, single spaced) than the writers spent writing them. No time left for anything else. Fortunately, I had a fallback job, so I stopped.

You were sixty in 2008. Where were you? What were you up to?

My father died in 2008 at the age of eighty-nine. That summer my beautiful California became an inferno, forest fires raging up and down the state. I wrote a story called "California Burning" about my dad and his cremation. Fire is a prominent theme. Also aliens, who somehow snuck their way in.

We did a staged reading of the story, harking back to my theater days. Big fun. You played one of the aliens, Terry. Remember? Everyone thought you were Terry Bisson, but we knew better.

The story's been optioned for a movie. My advice to you: stay by the phone.

Each in one sentence, please: Arthur C. Clarke, Molly Gloss, Atul Gawande.

Clarke: He had me at *2001*. But deep sea diving? A life underwater? The space elevator?!

Gloss: Stunning. Soulful. Not a wasted word.

Gawande: I haven't read him. I know, I know . . . and I do read widely in the field, but almost exclusively in professional journals.

You wrote a play, No Fast Dancing. *Was it performed?*

I was commissioned to write a play for an evening of Grand Guignol theater. *No Fast Dancing* was the result. Was it ever performed? I wish I knew. I've had work performed on stage, including short stories, that I only found out about afterwards.

You wrote a screenplay, Decodings. *Was it produced?*

Decodings is a groundbreaking independent film of found footage. Michael Wallin, the filmmaker, asked me to write the script, which I did. The film received a number of awards, including the Special Jury Award of the San Francisco Film Festival. It was also selected by the Whitney Museum for its biennial exhibit of American art.

What aspect of medicine interests you the most? Of writing?

Of medicine: our body's extraordinary and ongoing balancing act, its nearly flawless internal communication network, its deep ecology and multiple layers of consciousness. In the office, the most interesting stuff, not to mention the highest high, comes face to face, when a patient and I connect.

Of writing: rewriting. Digging.

A lot of writers deal with pain, psychological, spiritual, existential. You work deals with it as a medical event. You even suggest that it has a therapeutic function. Is this a scientific or a literary device?

Pain is universal. Every creature on earth reacts to it. It teaches us, human creatures, what to avoid. Internally, it alerts us that something's not right. Without pain we wouldn't survive.

In conditions where pain is blunted or absent, like diabetes, leprosy, drug and alcohol overdoses, injuries go unnoticed and can lead to infections that also go unnoticed, and these can lead to loss of limb, or worse.

For several years in the 1950s, prefrontal lobotomy was used for intractable pain. Cancer pain, for example. A last resort. The procedure involves severing the nerves that transmit pain from the lower to the upper brain. A funny thing happens when you do this. The patient continues to be aware of the pain but is no longer bothered by it. One is conscious but unperturbed.

This advanced the thinking about pain. A distinction was made between pain and suffering. The two could be detached, severed as it were.

Therapeutically, this can be useful. People can be triaged. This one, to physical therapy; that one, to psychological or emotional therapy. Some people benefit from both.

Pain is a fact of life. We've all experienced it, each of us in our own unique, self-defined way. I'm tempted to say the same about suffering, but I'm less sure. Personally, I've suffered, and professionally I've seen my share of it. But then I'll come across a patient who by all rights should be suffering terribly but isn't. Suffering somehow isn't in their DNA.

There's a saying I've heard, a kind of teaching: pain is inevitable, but suffering is optional. I think I understand what this is driving at, and it may be true. Or the truth may be more complicated, because our brains are complicated and only rarely severed.

True or not, it's a pretty high bar, if you ask me. But who doesn't like a person who meets adversity with pluck and courage?

Literature is full of such characters, including some of my own. They're among my favorites.

Anything new coming out?

All I Ever Dreamed, a collection (in a single volume) of all my stories and novellas since the ones that appeared in *The Brains of Rats*, from Valancourt Books.

A new novella, entitled *Longer*, about everything under the sun. Under *my* sun, that is: love, sex, gender, betrayal, forgiveness, a mysterious life form, weird experiments, life after death and death after life, space travel (yes, space travel), olfactory suspense, and more. The usual stuff, in other words. Lots of fun.

What kind of car do you drive? I ask this of everyone. Actually you can ignore this question, since I know you drive a car that initiates little discussion, which is perhaps its signal virtue.

Little discussion, save from my kids, who ridicule it mercilessly. Smelly and ugly, dented and scratched. But as it ages, so do they, and with age comes wisdom. In their case, an appreciation of the fact that the more they laugh, the less likely I am to trade it in.

Your work is concerned a lot with ethical dilemmas. Is this a feature of medicine or of science in general?

Science is amoral. You can't pick and choose. Or you can, but then you run a big risk. It's like free speech.

Medicine is not inherently ethical, any more than an individual is, or an institution is, or society is. All of them have an opinion and a say, not to mention a stake, in what is right and wrong.

Personally, I never *stop* thinking about ethical behavior. After I wrote my Reagan story, a man noted for his casual disregard for the sick and needy, I asked myself: if he were shot and came to me for help, would I give it? More to the point, could I refuse?

In practice, medicine should—and mostly does—make ethical decisions. But beware of unintended consequences.

Recently, under sustained pressure from PETA and other groups, the last medical school still using animals to train students stopped the practice. This was a victory, not just for the animals, not just for the animal rights activists, but for all of us who believe that life is precious, life of all kinds, that it's wrong to unnecessarily kill other species.

Ethically, this represented a step forward. No more animals sacrificed for the benefit of budding surgeons. Now these surgeons will do their practicing on people.

If you have money, you'll go to a surgeon with experience. If not, you'll get one of the others, who, in the absence of a dog or a sheep, will do their learning on you.

You say much of your medical practice is with the underserved. How does this work in the real world?

Except for one year in private practice, I've spent my whole career working in public, not-for-profit institutions, doing primary care. For four years I worked in a federally funded clinic in the Mission District of San Francisco, caring for immigrants, refugees, and the very poor.

For fifteen years after that I worked in an acute care clinic at UCSF, caring for roughly that same population.

My Jeopardy *item—I provide the answer, you provide the question. Answer: Gender.*

Question: Do you have time for this?

Medicine called to me from an early age.

Later, theater called, then music, then writing.

Somewhere between my first published story and my second, a memory called. I was holding the latest *Superman* comic in my hands. I was twelve or thirteen. The cover showed a big chunk of red kryptonite, which did weird and unexpected things to Superman, unlike green kryptonite, which was lethal. The red kryptonite issues were my favorites, and from my very first glance I knew this one would be my favorite of all time. Something really weird happened to Superman in this one. Really bizarre.

He turned into a woman.

I remember little else. I know he found a way to get rid of the red kryptonite, because he always did.

The question to me: why not, just this once, keep it around?

I started cross-dressing by accident. I was on a cruise with my best friend. We were thirteen or fourteen, the only boys on the ship. There was a costume party, and a fun-loving French newlywed decided she needed two female consorts. She dolled us up. I remember being titillated and nervous. When I look at the photo now, I am struck by how happy and natural I look.

I didn't dress up again for many years. When I did, it wasn't easy. Nothing fit. I wasn't into shopping yet, and my roommate's dresses were too small. When I tried them on, the seams ripped. Later on, I moved into an apartment of my own and became friends with the woman upstairs, who was extra-large. I had the key to her back door and would sometimes let myself in when she was at work. Her knee-high leather boots fit perfectly. This was a revelation, and a turning point, for me.

The cross-dressers I met in person, like the incredible Charles Ludlam, or on screen, like the beautiful and utterly convincing Harlow in *The Queen*, were gay. I wasn't gay. I wasn't precisely hetero, but those were the choices back then. When gay men came on to me, which happened with regularity, I was apologetic, while feeling misunderstood. When I later learned that the majority of cross-dressing men are heterosexual, I understood myself better.

As a transvestite I was lucky in all sorts of ways. I never judged myself harshly for who I was, or what I did, or fantasized doing. I was comfortable in my body and my skin. I liked dressing up. I liked having sex and saw nothing wrong having it in whatever way was fun. I was never hurt, and I never hurt anyone else.

Actually, I was hurt once, but not badly. I prostituted myself, not for money but for the experience. It was intense. I don't regret doing it, but I'm glad I didn't do it a second time.

I was a shy TV and kept to the shadows. After a while I got up the nerve to appear in public: it was the first and last time I did. That embarrassing.

I chose Halloween, which in San Francisco, if you weren't a flamboyant queen but instead a shrinking violet like me, was the night to come out of the closet. Come out I did.

I made two mistakes. One, I unwittingly chose to reveal myself at a hetero ball, *the* hetero Halloween ball, where women and men were dressed to the nines and looking for action, hetero action exclusively. This was a time of low awareness, not to mention tolerance, for hybrid creatures. Plus, I wasn't there for action; all I wanted was to be seen.

Two, I did my own hair, makeup, and clothes. Fine in the privacy of one's home. Inadvisable, as any fashion magazine on earth will tell you, for galas, soirees, and coming out parties.

I doubt I fooled anyone, though mercifully it was dark. Mostly, I was ignored, which was a blessing. At the end of the evening a kind woman took pity on me and handed me a long-stemmed rose, as you might to a sad, pathetic homeless person. I felt brave for having gone, and brave for having stayed, but in the moment mostly what I felt was awful.

It could have been so much worse, but as I said, I was lucky. I was lucky to live in the city I did. I was lucky in having friends who understood, or at least humored me. I was (and am) lucky for having a wife who, after the initial shock, was all in.

I was lucky not to get AIDS. I was lucky to live to the twenty-first century and a time when gender identity is understood to be not one thing, not fixed, but fluid and freewheeling, as it most certainly is.

Bibliography

Novels

The Roberts (Tachyon, 2011)
The Healer (Pyr Press, 2005)
X, Y (Dell, 1993)
The Movement of Mountains (St. Martin's, 1987)

Collections

What the Doctor Ordered (Tachyon, 2014)
The Brains of Rats (Scream Press, 1990; Dell, 1999)

Stories

"Y(ou)r Q(ua)ntifi(e)d S(el)f," *New Scientist*, no. 3000, December
    2014. (The unabridged original version will be found in the
    collection *All I Ever Dreamed*, Valancourt Books, 2018.)
"Choose Poison, Choose Life," *Asimov's Science Fiction* 40, no.
    10–11, October–November 2016

"Success," *Fantasy & Science Fiction* 125, no. 5–6, November–December 2013

"Bird Walks in New England," *Asimov's Science Fiction* 36, no. 7, July 2012

"Twenty-Two and You," *Fantasy & Science Fiction* 122, no. 3–4, March–April 2012

"California Burning," *Asimov's Science Fiction* 33, no. 8, August 2009

"The Big One," *Flurb*, no. 6, Fall/Winter 2008

"The Roberts," *Fantasy & Science Fiction* 115, no. 1, July 2008

"Strategy for Conflict Avoidance: Memo to the Commander-in-Chief," *Flurb*, no. 1, Fall 2006

"Greedy for Kisses," *Darkness Rising* (*Rolling Darkness Revue* 2005) anthology (Earthling Press), 2005

"Know How, Can Do," *Fantasy & Science Fiction* 101, no. 6, December 2001

"Fidelity: A Primer," *Fantasy & Science Fiction* 99, no. 3, September 2000

"Isostasy," MichaelBlumlein.com, 1999

"Revenge," *Fantasy & Science Fiction* 94, no. 4, April 1998

"Paul and Me," *Fantasy & Science Fiction* 93, no. 4–5, October–November 1997

"Snow in Dirt," *Black Swan, White Raven* (Ellen Datlow & Terri Windling, editors), Avon, 1997

"Bloom," *Interzone*, no. 94, April 1995

"Hymenoptera," *Dark Love* (Collins, Kramer, and Greenberg, eds.), Roc, 1995; *Crank!*, no. 1, 1993

"The Wet Suit," *The Brains of Rats* collection, 1990

"The Glitter and the Glamour," *The Brains of Rats* collection, 1990

"Bestseller," *Fantasy & Science Fiction* 78, no. 1, January 1990

"Keeping House," *The Brains of Rats* collection, 1990

"Shed His Grace," *Semiotext(e) SF* 5, no. 2, 1989

"The Promise of Warmth," *Twilight Zone* 8, no. 3, August 1988

"The Domino Master," *Omni* 10, no. 9, June 1988

"Interview with C.W.," *New Pathways*, no. 10, March 1988

"Drown Yourself," *Mississippi Review* 16, no. 2–3, 1988

"The Thing Itself," *Full Spectrum* anthology (Bantam Spectra), 1988

"Softcore," *Processed World*, no. 20, September 1987

"The Brains of Rats," *Interzone*, no. 16, Summer 1986

"Tissue Ablation and Variant Regeneration: A Case Report,"
      Interzone, no. 7, Spring 1984

About the Author

MICHAEL BLUMLEIN, MD, IS a native of San Francisco. In addition to his acclaimed science fiction, he has written for the stage and for film.

His novel *X,Y* was made into a feature-length movie. He wrote the screenplay for *Decodings*, which was selected for inclusion in the Biennial Exhibition of the Whitney Museum of American Art (1989). In 2011 he was one of a panel of experts at the "Impossible Futures" symposium sponsored by the Institute for the Future in Silicon Valley.

His stories have been widely anthologized and taught in a variety of settings, including high schools, colleges, and medical and law schools.

In addition to writing, Dr. Blumlein is a practicing MD and a faculty member at the University of California in San Francisco. Much of his career has been spent caring for the underserved.

FRIEND OF

PM

These are indisputably momentous times—the financial system is melting down globally and the Empire is stumbling. Now more than ever there is a vital need for radical ideas.

In the years since its founding—and on a mere shoestring—PM Press has risen to the formidable challenge of publishing and distributing knowledge and entertainment for the struggles ahead. With hundreds of releases to date, we have published an impressive and stimulating array of literature, art, music, politics, and culture. Using every available medium, we've succeeded in connecting those hungry for ideas and information to those putting them into practice.

Friends of PM allows you to directly help impact, amplify, and revitalize the discourse and actions of radical writers, filmmakers, and artists. It provides us with a stable foundation from which we can build upon our early successes and provides a much-needed subsidy for the materials that can't necessarily pay their own way. You can help make that happen—and receive every new title automatically delivered to your door once a month—by joining as a Friend of PM Press. And, we'll throw in a free T-shirt when you sign up.

Here are your options:

- **$30 a month**: Get all books and pamphlets plus 50% discount on all webstore purchases
- **$40 a month**: Get all PM Press releases (including CDs and DVDs) plus 50% discount on all webstore purchases
- **$100 a month**: Superstar—Everything plus PM merchandise, free downloads, and 50% discount on all webstore purchases

For those who can't afford $30 or more a month, we have Sustainer Rates at $15, $10, and $5. Sustainers get a free PM Press T-shirt and a 50% discount on all purchases from our website.

Your Visa or Mastercard will be billed once a month, until you tell us to stop. Or until our efforts succeed in bringing the revolution around. Or the financial meltdown of Capital makes plastic redundant. Whichever comes first.

PM Press was founded at the end of 2007 by a small collection of folks with decades of publishing, media, and organizing experience. PM Press co-conspirators have published and distributed hundreds of books, pamphlets, CDs, and DVDs. Members of PM have founded enduring book fairs, spearheaded victorious tenant organizing campaigns, and worked closely with bookstores, academic conferences, and even rock bands to deliver political and challenging ideas to all walks of life. We're old enough to know what we're doing and young enough to know what's at stake.

We seek to create radical and stimulating fiction and nonfiction books, pamphlets, T-shirts, visual and audio materials to entertain, educate, and inspire you. We aim to distribute these through every available channel with every available technology—whether that means you are seeing anarchist classics at our bookfair stalls; reading our latest vegan cookbook at the café; downloading geeky fiction e-books; or digging new music and timely videos from our website.

PM Press is always on the lookout for talented and skilled volunteers, artists, activists, and writers to work with. If you have a great idea for a project or can contribute in some way, please get in touch.

PM Press
PO Box 23912
Oakland CA 94623
510-658-3906
www.pmpress.org